CHRISTMAS INN MAINE

CHELSEA M. CAMERON

Get Free Books

Tropetastic romance with a twist, Happily Ever Afters guaranteed! You can expect humor and heart in every Chelsea M. Cameron romance.

Get a free book today! Join Chelsea's Newsletter and get a copy of Marriage of Unconvenience, about two best friends who get fake married to share an inheritance and end up with a lot of *real* feelings.

And now, back to Christmas Inn Maine…

About Christmas Inn Maine

All Colden Hayes wanted was to spend Christmas by herself in a cottage by the sea where the cheer of the holiday season couldn't reach her. Everything was going according to plan until the cottage she rented turned out not to exist and she ends up snowed in at a charming inn that happens to be owned by the family of her most-hated coworker, Laura Sterling. Talk about bad luck.

Colden ends up saying yes to Laura's mother when she insists on giving her a room. It's only for a night, but she somehow finds herself agreeing to spend Christmas with the Sterlings as well. She blamed the festive atmosphere that she couldn't seem to escape. Maybe there's something in the mistletoe?

Against her will, Colden finds herself being sucked into the comfort and joy of the season, even though she can't seem to escape Laura, who is literally everywhere Colden is, like she's doing it on purpose. Things get even worse when they're forced to share a bed when there's a fire at a local farm and the inn offers all the available rooms to the family.

Colden finally realizes there's a thin line between annoyance and attraction, and she and Laura definitely crossed it. She's also pretty sure that Laura's mother is shipping them hard and so is the rest of her family, right down to her great-grandmother whose main companion is a two-hundred-pound pig named Minnie.

Will the magic of the holiday season melt Colden's heart? Or will she go back to Boston alone, with only the memories to keep her warm?

Chapter One

IF SOMEONE CALLED me a grinch one more time, I was going to lose my shit. So what, I hated Christmas. Was that a crime now?

"So you're going to be *alone?*" my coworker, Betty, said with horror on her face, as if I'd said I was going to murder and dismember a litter of puppies.

"Yes," I said, through gritted teeth. Betty shook her head and made disappointed noises with her mouth while I tried not to scream.

"That just doesn't seem right. Christmas is for family." I didn't feel like explaining to her that my mom had run off and abandoned me and dad, and that he'd died a few years ago and I was an only child with relatives that didn't really care about my existence. It was kind of a conversational downer, so I just let people believe that I was a bitter bitch who hated joy and togetherness.

I was distracted from dealing with Betty by the arrival of a person who annoyed me even more than she did: Laura. Just thinking her name made me want to snarl.

"Hey, did you finish those subs yet?" she asked me, tossing

her long spiral-curled brown locks over her shoulder. Laura was the kind of girl who could wear her hair down all the time and it always looked perfect. Mine was up constantly, today in a lazy braid.

"I will this afternoon," I said, as Betty went back to her desk. All I wanted was to drink my coffee in peace, but no. Laura couldn't let me do that with her perfect hair and her heeled boots that made a clicking sound on the linoleum.

"Great, I just wanted to remind you so you didn't forget."

"I won't," I said, my voice thick with fake cheerfulness. Either Laura didn't notice, or she chose to ignore it, as she thanked me and went back to her desk.

We both worked at a small literary agency in Boston as assistants to the head literary agent. My goal was to work my way up and maybe get to New York, if I could ever save up enough to afford it.

I thought about having another cup of coffee to make it through the afternoon, but instead I went for some tea. I was trying to be better about having too much caffeine in the afternoon. I glopped some honey into my cup and braced myself to go back to my desk. It was right next to Laura's, which was just . . . not great.

Fortunately, she kept her head down most of the time, but that also worked against me because if she worked hard, I had to work twice as hard. I fell short a lot.

This was a competitive industry and she was my competition and my enemy. I had heard through the grapevine (Betty and her big mouth), that one of the junior agents might be moving to New York, and her position would be open. I wanted it, and I knew Laura would too.

It was ON.

First up was getting through these last submissions. Our boss, Ping, had already left for the holidays (as most of publishing did in the month of December), but here Laura and

I were, along with the rest of the lower rungs on the ladder, still working our butts off to get through the backlog of submissions. Everyone and their uncle thought they had The Great American Novel in them, and it was my job to sort through the garbage and find a diamond to show Ping.

I'd discarded everything so far today, and I was hoping to have one that I wanted to show her when she got back, but it wasn't looking promising.

"Anything good?" a voice asked from behind me, and I almost had a heart attack.

"No," I said, as I tried to calm my heart. "And you shouldn't lurk like that, it's creepy." Laura had the habit of reading over my shoulder, yet another thing that made her the most annoying person on the planet.

"Bummer. They today, huh?" she said, pointing at my pronoun pin that had THEY/THEM printed on it.

"Yeah," I said. The one thing that could be said for Laura was that she always respected my pronouns, at least to my face.

"Cool," she said, and went back to her desk. I wasn't sure what the point of that interruption had been, except to show me how good her hair looked when she tossed it over her shoulder like she was in a shampoo commercial.

I went back to reading submissions and put in my earbuds so I could block out the noise of the rest of the office. Just three more days of work until I was off for two whole weeks. I was out-of-my-mind excited. I'd rented a cottage on the coast of Maine and I couldn't wait to get there and not talk to anyone for the duration of my trip. It was going to be heaven. I'd already planned out my reading schedule to the hour and packed my books in my car. A cottage by the sea called for reading physical books, as far as I was concerned.

I made it through the rest of the day and decided to clock out. Laura was still working while I gathered my stuff up to leave, but I was going to let her have this one.

"See you tomorrow," I said, as I wrapped myself in my jacket, hat, scarf, and gloves. Boston winter winds could be brutal. Strip the skin right off your face.

"Bye," she said, her eyes glued to the screen. She'd recently gotten some of those glasses that were supposed to help block the blue light from computers and they looked really good on her, which was totally annoying. I wore contacts because I looked goofy with glasses on, but she looked like a freaking model.

I headed out to the freezing, icy sidewalk and headed toward the train. I was lucky to live only a few stops away from work. I wasn't so lucky that I had to live with someone else, but my roommate was fine. She did her thing, I did mine, and we rarely interacted. She worked nights as a nurse and slept during the day, so it was pretty ideal.

She'd already left when I got home, so I had the kitchen to myself to make a quick dinner and grabbing my eating book. I had different books for different activities and moods. A dinner book was one I could have in front of my face and eat with one hand and not have to focus on too much. I read a little bit at a time. These were most often my re-reads.

Post-dinner books were new releases, or books that I really wanted to finish. Pre-bed books had to be soothing, so I didn't stay up all night. I also didn't allow myself to start a new book within an hour of going to bed. That had bitten me in the ass one too many times before.

Before I started my post-dinner book, I checked out the listing for my cottage again. I'd even bought long underwear and pajamas with lobsters on them. I was going to make a bunch of soup and stare at the snow and read with mugs of hot cider warming my hands.

This was going to be my new Christmas tradition, after forcing myself to try and fit in for years. This Christmas would be mine, and mine alone.

I COUNTED DOWN the moments until I could reasonably leave on Friday.

"Got somewhere to go?" Laura asked.

"Yup," I said, my knees jiggling in anticipation under my desk as I watched the seconds tick down.

"What are your holiday plans?" she asked.

"Being alone," I said. I hadn't told anyone exactly where I was going, just that I was going away.

"Oh," she said, and I could feel her wanting to ask more, but she didn't. I finally clocked out and nearly skipped to the door.

"Uh, have a good holiday. See you," I said. I didn't stay to see if she replied. I was OUT of here.

IT STARTED SNOWING as I drove up I-95 and into the state of Maine. I'd always had an affinity for Maine, but hadn't been here much. I finally headed off the highway and stopped to get enough food to feed me for two weeks and ignored everyone else who was all hopped up on holiday energy.

"Are you sure about this?" I said to my GPS as it told me I'd arrived at my destination a half-hour later.

"You have arrived," the robotic voice said, but there was no cabin here. I peered through the falling snow, which had gotten thicker as I'd driven. Usually, when it snowed in Boston, I would just park my car in a local garage so I wouldn't have to clean it off and then just use public transportation. I didn't mess around with that shit. I probably should have looked at the weather or thought about this ahead of time. At least I had snow tires so I wasn't going to end up in a ditch, but as I stared out at the empty lot where my beautiful cottage was supposed to be, I was wishing I'd stayed in Boston.

Fuck.

"Fuck!" I yelled, and slammed my hands against the steering wheel. I got on the app where I'd booked the cottage and tried to find a contact number, something. All I got was a "live chat" that was wholly unhelpful and just told me to cancel and rebook and they'd "look into it." No contact info for the people I was supposed to be renting from. Just an email. I tried that, but I wasn't going to hold my breath.

I was completely fucked. I'd have to go back to Boston and see if I could somehow get my money back for the imaginary cottage. I didn't particularly feel like driving back in this, but what else was I going to do?

Panicking a little, I started driving slowly in the snow, looking for . . . I don't know. Anything. Anyone. Someone to save me.

A black iron sign loomed out of the whiteness: THE STERLING INN. It was perfect. As if it had appeared just for me. I pulled into the drive and parked in the lot. The inn was a lovely white farmhouse with a red barn. They must do a lot of weddings here in the summer.

I got out of my car and walked up the front porch of the inn and through the double doors that were hung with wreaths. It was like stepping right into a postcard.

The inside was warm, with a cozy fireplace to my left and a desk to my right. I stomped off my boots in the entry so I didn't get snow all over the plush rugs covering the hardwood floors that creaked just a little when you walked, as if they were original.

Garland hung from the bannisters of a staircase that had probably seen its fair share of grand entrances, and I counted at least five fully decked Christmas trees in the entry. They didn't mess around here.

"Can I help you?" a voice said to my right at the desk.

"Oh, yes, uh, I am in a bit of a pickle. I was supposed to be renting a cottage, but uh, the cottage doesn't exist. Have you heard of this?" I pulled the listing up on my phone and showed it to her.

"No, I'm sorry. That doesn't look like a place I recognize. Do you need a room?"

I was just about to say that I did and cringe at the cost when something hit me in the back of my legs.

"Minnie, no!"

I almost fell over as I turned to see what the hell was happening, and I swore I saw . . .

"Is that a pig?" I asked, as something large and round and black ran through to the dining room with someone right behind it.

"Yes, that's Minnie," the front desk person said with a rueful smile. "She's part of the family."

"Family?" I asked, turning back to her as the echo of squeals faded away.

"Yes, the Sterling family."

"Sterling family?" I asked.

"Yes, we, I mean, they, own the inn. I'm just cheap labor because I'm related. I'm Michelle Sterling," she said.

"Uh, yeah. How much is it going to be?"

"Let's see," she said, going to a computer monitor.

"We don't have a ton of availability, but The Nautical Suite is available at three fifty a night, and there's also The Schooner Room for three hundred."

I closed my eyes and counted to five so I didn't scream. This little Christmas trip was really going to pile on the credit card debt.

"Would you like to see the rooms before you decide?" Michelle asked.

"Sure, yeah, that sounds great." I put a smile on my face

and tried to suck it up. Hey, at least I was going to spend a night at this gorgeous inn. Hopefully one of the rooms had a bathtub I could soak my whole body in.

Michelle took me upstairs and I saw even more charm. There were photographs of people everywhere, which Michelle pointed out as various Sterlings.

"We've lived in this town for generations. We all live within a few miles of each other." That was probably supposed to sound heartwarming, but I shuddered and she laughed.

"It's not always bad. We always have interesting people around. And Portland isn't that far away." I couldn't imagine living this isolated, even if it was close to the beach.

Michelle showed me The Schooner room, which was fine, but then we went to The Nautical Suite and I was ready to throw myself on the California King canopy bed in the bedroom. There was also a little sitting room and a small kitchen area with a hot plate, a microwave, and a small fridge. Plus, the bathroom had a Jacuzzi tub that I was going to spend at least an hour in.

"I'll take it," I said, putting my bag down on a chair.

"Great. I'll just run your card information. Do you need any help with your luggage?" I wasn't going to need all my books for just staying a night, but I didn't want to leave them in the car, so I said, "Yeah, that would be good."

A surly teenage boy huffed my suitcase full of books up the stairs, along with the rest of my luggage, into my room. He just stood there waiting and I wanted to ask if there was something wrong with him, but he was waiting for a tip. I just happened to have some cash in my wallet, so I gave him a fiver and that seemed to do the trick.

He shut the door behind him and I flopped on the bed. So, maybe this wasn't a complete loss. If I wasn't so fucking broke, I might consider staying here for Christmas. They'd probably haul me downstairs to sing carols and eat gingerbread cookies, though, so it was probably for the best.

The room was so pretty, done in shades of light and dark blue and cream, with pictures of knots as well as two lamps that were made from giant knots on the dark blue nightstands. It was so classic and so Maine and I adored it. There was even a fucking rocking chair with a pillow that had blue knots printed on the fabric.

I realized I was starving. They'd just started serving dinner in the dining room, and it seemed silly to order room service since I could walk my ass downstairs.

I left the beautiful room and went downstairs. There were already a few people in the dinning room, including an older woman who might be sixty and might be three hundred and the most enormous black pig I'd seen in my life. Not that I'd seen a lot of pigs. She was feeding it scraps from the table like a dog. That was something I definitely hadn't seen in my life.

"Granny, you can't do that," I heard a familiar voice say, and I turned to see none other than Laura. The coworker I'd seen yesterday. I stood there gaping for a second, sure this was a mirage. She couldn't possibly be here, at this random Maine inn. What the fuck? It had to be someone who looked like her.

Then the pig turned around, saw me, and ran over. I put my hands up to protect myself, but it skidded to a stop right in front of me and looked up, making soft noises.

"Uh, hello?" I said, unsure of what to do. Did you pet pigs like dogs? What was pig etiquette?

"Colden?" the raspy voice said, and I looked from the pig to the approaching Laura. Yup, definitely her.

"What the fuck are you doing here?" I said as the pig wiggled in front of me as if it wanted me to do something.

"This is my family's inn," she said, looking just as stunned as I probably did. Her face had gotten pale.

"Oh," I said, because what else was there to say?

"She wants you to pet her," she said, pointing at the pig. "Right on the top of her head or under her chin."

This was the most bizarre moment of my entire life, and that was saying a lot.

"Your last name is Sterling," I said, finally making the connection.

"Yeah," she said, leaning down to pet the pig. "What are *you* doing here?"

"I was supposed to rent a cottage that turned out not to exist and there was a lot of snow and now I'm here and you're petting a pig."

"Yes, I am," she said, and I could feel her irritation. I wasn't too happy either.

"I should go," I said, but one look outside told me that my car wasn't headed anywhere.

"No, it's fine. I'll stay out of your way. Go, have dinner." She grabbed the pig's collar and tried to drag it back to the table with the older woman, but the pig wasn't going to go. The thing weighed several hundred pounds at least.

"Will you just pet her so she'll be happy?" Laura said, still struggling with the pig.

"Okay?" I said. I leaned down and scratched the top of the pig's head. It was dry and covered in wiry little hairs. Not exactly soft, but the pig made little happy noises and wagged its tail like a dog.

After a few moments, the pig dashed back to the table, as if satisfied.

"She has to greet everyone who comes in here whether they want to greet her or not," Laura said. "Excuse me." She left and I realized she had a white shirt, black pants, black apron, and black bowtie on. The dining staff uniform.

Did I want to hop in my car and risk death rather than sit down and be waited on by Laura? Yes. Did I? No.

I sat down at a damn table and she came over to fill my water glass and give me a menu.

"The specials today are the lobster pot pie, the fennel, cranberry, and goat cheese salad, and the cinnamon bread pudding," she said in a robotic voice, not even looking at me. "Can I start you with something to drink?"

I thought about saying "alcohol" but told her I wanted a glass of Cabernet and after a quick perusal of the menu, I ordered all of the specials.

She snatched my menu away and I glanced out the window at the snow. It was really coming down in white clouds. The backyard of the inn was lit up, including the gazebo and, if it weren't fucking freezing out there, it would be pretty beautiful to sit and read for a while. At least I had my books back up in my room. Should have brought one down with me, but I had hundreds on my phone, so I pulled up one of my dinner books and started reading while I waited for the wine.

Laura arrived with the glass and set it down in front of me. She looked even more pissed than she'd been when she took my menu.

"Your salad will be right out." She left me and made her rounds to the other tables and I watched her. I'd never seen her with her hair up, and it was throwing me off. Did her parents own this inn? Was she going to inherit? I didn't really know her story because I'd never asked.

I saw her go to the table with the older woman and the pig, and there were a few other people sitting there. Laura leaned down to one woman who wore a suit so well she looked like she belonged in a city, and not at this charming small-town inn.

The woman looked over at me and our eyes locked and I knew she had to be Laura's mother. They were practically twins. The mother looked at Laura and then back at me before getting up and making her way over to my table.

Shit. I shouldn't have been staring.

I looked into my wine glass. I'd been so distracted by Laura I hadn't touched it yet.

Laura followed the woman who was definitely her mother and I wished I had a book in front of my face to avoid them, but I was out of luck.

"Hello, I'm Laina Sterling. Laura tells me that you work together. It's so lovely to meet you." She put her perfectly manicured, ring-studded hand out and I had no choice but to shake it.

"Uh, hi. Yes, we work together."

"What brings you to Maine?" Laina asked, and Laura had to go tend to another table, leaving me alone with her mother. I wanted to slip through a crack in the floor and disappear forever. Why was this happening to me?

"I, um, rented a cottage, and it didn't work out and it was snowing so I stopped here for the night and I'll drive back to Boston when the snow stops." I didn't really feel like chatting with Laura's mother. This whole thing was awkward enough without me getting drawn into her family.

The dining room started to fill up with other people and I hoped she would move on and go talk with someone else.

"Oh, you don't need to leave. Stay. We have plenty of room." Now I was in the position of telling her there wasn't enough room on my credit card for more nights at this place.

"As our guests, of course. On the house." My mouth almost dropped open at the offer.

"No, no, that's fine. I couldn't possibly accept that. I've got plans back in Boston." She looked at me and I could tell she knew I had no plans.

"It's no imposition. We have plenty of other family staying here right now at no charge. What's one more?" Wow, guess they didn't really care about making enough money from their rooms. They probably made enough the rest of the year, but that didn't mean I wanted to be their charity case.

"Listen, have dinner and think about it. It's no trouble at all. The more, the merrier." She patted my arm and got up. I sputtered and couldn't form any words and she swept away before I could come up with anything to say. Then Laura was back with my salad. Her lips were pressed together and her jaw was tight as she set the plate down. I expected her to head off again, but she paused.

"What did my mom say to you?" I stabbed a piece of salad with my fork.

"She asked me to stay longer. For free. Don't worry, I'll be out of your hair tomorrow, as soon as I can." She tapped her foot on the floor and crossed her arms.

"I'm not going to stay," I reiterated. "I don't want to be here anymore than you want me here." She seemed to get increasingly agitated at my presence. I'd never really seen her like this at the office. She must keep the hostility under wraps when our boss was around.

"Whatever," she said, and then walked off. Okay, then.

The salad was amazing and I finished my first glass of wine before I was done with my salad and was feeling pleasantly warm and cozy. I sunk into the gentle sounds of silverware on plates and chatter. Halfway through the dinner, someone sat down at the grand piano at the other end of the dining room and started playing softly. Against my will, I was charmed by the whole place. The wine was partially to blame, I hoped.

My potpie came and was one of the most delicious things I'd ever eaten, but I would have rather eaten glass than tell Laura how good it was when she came and asked. I sipped at a second glass of wine and waited for my dessert. The dining room had gotten louder as the evening progressed and the piano player struck up a tune and all of a sudden, everyone was singing. I looked around and found a red-faced Laura looking like she wanted to die. I snorted into my napkin. I might as well enjoy this while I was here. I could bring it up again and tease her with it when she pissed me off at work.

I almost started singing along, since I knew the tune. It was one of my dad's favorites.

This place was really doing a number on me. I needed to get out ASAP. I finished my dessert and waited for the bill. Laura came back over and asked how everything was and I couldn't lie.

"Excellent." I waited for her to give me the check. I had my card ready so it would be a quick process, but no bill was produced.

"Your dinner has been comped," she finally said.

"Oh, you didn't need to do that."

"I didn't. Take it up with my mother, but you'll lose. She always gets her way." She sighed and I almost wanted to know the story there. Laura looked off into the distance and I could tell she was stressed about this whole thing. It couldn't be easy to have someone you don't like invading your space.

"Well, she didn't need to do that, but thank her. I'm going to go back to my room and stay there the rest of the night so you won't see me again until I'm leaving tomorrow." I scurried from the table before she could say anything else.

I had plans for the rest of the night, and they involved the Jacuzzi tub, some bath oil, a robe, and plenty of guilt-free TV. Might as well enjoy it because tomorrow it was back to Boston and back to my real life. I hadn't heard from the renter of the imaginary cottage, but the booking site said they were looking into things and I was probably going to get a refund since I cancelled the booking. It would just take some time to process, so I wasn't completely fucked.

I found some battery candles and set them up and made a whole spa atmosphere in the bathroom before sinking into the tub and filling it with water and lavender bath oil. Perfection.

I let the water melt (most of) my stress away and then

wrapped myself in a thick robe and climbed into the giant bed. Someday, I wanted to have a bed this big. Someday, I wanted to have an apartment that would fit a bed this big.

After a while, I started feeling like I wanted a little something, and found that they did have room service until ten. The menu was limited, but they did have an assorted cookie plate that came with a glass of milk. Fuck yeah, that's what I wanted. I called down and ended up speaking with Michelle and placing the order. I told her not to comp it, but to put it on my card.

"I'm sorry, I can't. My aunt makes the rules and you're not allowed to pay for anything. Sorry." She did seem apologetic about it.

"Then I'm cancelling my order. Sorry to bother you." I hung up before she could say anything else. I didn't want Laura holding this shit over my head at work.

Fifteen minutes later there was a knock at my door. I got up and made sure the robe was secure and looked through the peephole.

Laura stood there with a covered tray along with a huge glass and a pitcher of what was probably milk. I had no choice but to open the door.

"Your cookies and milk," she said, and I could feel the annoyance radiating off her again. Like, major annoyance.

"Don't you have a room service person?"

"Usually, but tonight that person is me." She shoved the tray at me and I had no choice but to accept it or drop it and lose all the precious cookies and spill milk that she'd probably have to clean up.

"You're not wearing your pin," she said as I struggled with the tray. I needed to get to the gym more. Build up my arms a little bit.

"No, I wasn't planning on being with people who would need to know my pronouns. She is good. I'll let you know if that changes." It was my default, but I still had they/them days and sometimes they/them weeks. Being a demigirl was confusing as fuck sometimes. Why couldn't I just have been given the right gender in the first place?

"Fine," she said, before pivoting and stomping down the hallway.

My cookies didn't taste as good as I wanted them to, and the milk was so ice cold it made my teeth hurt. I told myself that I wasn't going to let Laura affect my mood, but Laura was definitely affecting my mood.

Ugh, I didn't want to think about her. I flipped through the channels that were showing a hell of a lot of holiday content that I skipped and settled on the network that had the show about people buying houses. I finished the plate of cookies, which had included double chocolate chip, gingerbread, sugar, oatmeal chocolate chip, and these little ones that had jam sandwiched in between. Perfection.

I left the TV on and put on my pajamas and brushed my teeth. My alarm was set for much earlier than I wanted it to be, but I was going to have to dig my car out of the parking lot before I got on the road. Definitely wasn't looking forward to that. I settled into the bed and was nearly asleep when there was a commotion in the hallway that sounded like a stampede, urgent whispering, and a strange squealing noise.

The pig was loose.

Chapter Two

I DIDN'T THINK I'd be much help in catching the pig, so I stayed in bed, but I couldn't sleep. It wasn't just the strange room, although that was what I wanted to tell myself.

If I was being completely and totally honest: the idea of going back to Boston tomorrow was making me more depressed than I thought it would. I'd just gotten so excited about the little cottage by the sea.

Fuck, I still had all the damn groceries in my car. I'd completely forgotten about them in the back. At least it was cold enough that everything would stay frozen? Yet another waste.

I groaned and tried to find a comfortable sleeping position.

A book. I needed a book. I got up and went to the suitcase that had my books in it. I turned the light on in the little sitting area and looked through to find one of the books I'd picked to help me get to sleep.

There was a tiny coffeemaker in the room that also dispensed hot water and I scrounged up some peppermint tea and found a packet of honey. If I couldn't sleep, the next best thing was reading.

I pulled a soft cotton blanket off the back of the loveseat and curled up in it with the book and the steaming cup of tea beside me. Too bad I couldn't stay here for the next two weeks, but there were two big obstacles to that plan. Laura and money. I wasn't going to overcome either of those anytime soon, so even though it almost broke my heart, I was heading back to Boston in a few hours. I just had to kill some time until then and turned the page of my book.

THE NEXT TIME I AWOKE, I was still on the couch and the book had fallen to the floor. There were sounds outside the door of people bustling around and stepping on creaky floorboards and having conversations about coffee and pancakes and plans for the day.

I blinked and looked out the window. It had stopped snowing, finally, but there was definitely at least a foot or more piled up outside. The white gazebo was frosted with icicles hanging from the roof. It was disgusting how picturesque this place was.

I got up from the couch and groaned. It was a nice couch, but nothing could beat a bed for sleeping. Too bad I'd never get to find out what it was like to wake up in the California king. I sighed and packed my book up and threw on some clothes before brushing my teeth and packing the rest of my shit away.

I did want to have breakfast and thank Laina for letting me stay. I had the feeling they would have an incredible spread and I didn't want to miss it before I left.

I brushed out my tangled light-brown shoulder-length hair and made a face at the dark circles under my eyes. I wasn't winning any beauty contests today, but when did I ever? That was what was so freeing about being non-binary: I didn't have to fit into the traditional "beauty" box. Sure, I liked to lean on the femme side, but I also rarely wore any kind of makeup, and I only wore a dress once in a blue moon. Weirdly enough, I'd gotten a little obsessed with jewelry lately, like a magpie, and I'd been collecting statement necklaces and lots and lots of bracelets that I stacked up and down my arms.

I shoved on just about every one of my favorites. The jingling comforted me for some reason. I turned my head to the side and figured that was good enough.

The smells hit me the second I put my head out of the door and into the hallway. Bacon, cinnamon, fresh coffee, warm bread, and a million other spices and scents that made me instantly starving.

I slowly made my way downstairs and peeked into the dining room. Whole lotta people in there, including Laina, the pig, and Laura. I didn't know who I wanted to avoid more.

I tried to sneak in, but that didn't really work.

"Colden, good morning," Laina said, coming over. It was literally looking at what Laura would turn into in the future. Incredibly beautiful. Not as if she wasn't already, but age would only sharpen it and make it more intense, if that was possible.

"Good morning," I said through a yawn.

"Did you sleep well?" I shrugged.

"Oh, no, was there something wrong with the room?" She seemed genuinely concerned and it was making me embarrassed.

"No, just with my brain," I said, looking for a way out.

"I'm sorry about that, but you look like you could use a good breakfast. Why don't you come and sit with us?" For a second, I considered bolting and just heading for my car and leaving right then.

"Oh, no, that's fine. I should get on the road." So much for eating.

"Come and sit down," Laina said, putting her arm around

me and dragging me into the room. I wanted to dig my heels in, but I didn't. Instead of leading me to the cluster of tables that she'd come from, she took me to a little nook where there was a table that would only fit two people max and motioned for me to sit down.

"Is this better?" It wasn't ideal, but it was the best in the given situation. I was at the back of the dining room, so I could see all the activity, but was apart from it.

"Thank you," I said, and Laina gave me a warm smile and squeezed my shoulder.

"Enjoy your breakfast and don't you dare try to pay. My husband Antonio and I wouldn't hear of it and he's the chef." She pointed her finger at me and I wanted to argue, but you didn't argue with a woman like Laina Sterling.

She smiled and walked back out of the dining room. I sat there for a second and then Laura appeared. She was gorgeous, of course, but there were also dark circles under her eyes, and her shoulders were slumped a little.

"Do you want to know the specials?" she said with a sigh as she handed me a menu. I did, but I also didn't want to make her repeat them.

"No, that's fine," I said, looking at the menu.

"Can I start you with something to drink?" She had dropped all pretense of being happy I was here and I could tell if I stood up and walked out, she would be relieved.

"I'm leaving soon, I promise. I was just hungry."

She sighed again.

"I'll have a caramel latte and a glass of cranberry orange," I said, not looking up at her.

"Fine," she said and stomped away. She was probably going to spit in my juice.

While I tried to decide what I wanted to eat, I scanned the room and took it all in. Laina flitted around, talking and laughing with each table. I also saw Michelle a few times, and there was the pig with the older woman who wouldn't stop feeding it from the table. A little weird that they had bacon on the menu.

The warmth and coziness of the breakfast was seeping into my bones again. I realized I didn't want to leave. Then Laura came over with my coffee and juice and I reminded myself that I did need to leave.

"Ready to order?" she asked. I hadn't seen her write down a single order she'd taken and I had to admit that was pretty impressive. There were a few other servers to take care of the dining room, but she was the one who always seemed to be moving in three directions at once.

What had brought her to Boston and away from here? Why hadn't she stayed?

"Colden?" she said, snapping me out of my mental rambling.

"Yeah, sorry. I'm going to have the eggs benedict with a side of potatoes and the fruit. Thanks."

She took the menu and went to grab a coffee pot to give someone a refill before going to take another order. I pretended to mess with my phone, but I was watching Laura. I was tired just seeing all the things she was doing.

I wondered if she was getting paid, or if this was the "break" she got. Not exactly relaxing if you got roped into still working. That kind of sucked. No wonder she was tired.

I got lost in wondering about Laura and didn't notice until I heard a snuffling noise that the pig had wandered over to my table.

"Oh, hello." I was still a little uneasy about the giant animal, but it seemed friendly. Did pigs bite?

I scratched the top of the pig's head and then I heard a voice.

"Minnie likes you." I looked up to find the older woman beaming down at me.

"Minnie?" I asked.

"That's her name. She was supposed to be a miniature pig, but you can see how well that turned out." I looked into her face and saw Laura's and Laina's eyes. She smiled and her whole face crinkled in a way that made me want to smile with her.

"I'm Lillian," she said. "Laina is my granddaughter and Laura is my great-granddaughter." Holy shit. I had no idea how old she was, but if she was a great-grandmother she was probably up there. Her age was actually kind of intimidating.

"I'm Colden. I, uh, work with Laura, but that's not why I'm here. That's just a coincidence." I wasn't sure how much, if anything, Laura had told her about me. Probably nothing nice. It was surprising that they would be so nice to me.

"Well, it's so nice to meet one of Laura's friends from the big city. I haven't been to Boston in years."

I didn't correct her that I wasn't one of Laura's friends. "Do you mind if I sit down? The bones are giving me a hard time." She sat with a flop, and I worried she might tip over and fall right off the chair, but she got herself situated without incident.

"So, Colden, tell me about yourself." She leaned back in her chair and regarded me with those eyes that reminded me far too much of Laura. I'd never seen such a strong family resemblance before. Those were some strong genes.

"There's not much to tell?" I said, hoping that would be that. I had many methods to scare people from not asking too many personal questions about myself. I wondered how many I'd have to go through with Lillian before she'd give up.

"Oh, I don't believe that for a second. The most interesting people always turn out to be the ones who think they're the least interesting. Come now, indulge an old woman." She patted my hand and winked.

"You're not that old," I said, and the corners of her eyes crinkled in a smile.

"You're sassy, I like that. Now tell me where you come from, Colden." I didn't want to, but for some reason I started telling her that I was from just outside Boston and had always wanted to get to the big city, but hadn't been able to until college. Before she could ask about my parents, I told her that my mom had left me. I had no idea where she was and it didn't matter. I'd burned that bridge, drained the river, and salted the earth.

"I'm so sorry that she did that to you. No one deserves to have their mother leave like that." I appreciated her words and they almost made me want to cry. This was why I didn't talk about my parents.

Before I could get into the sob story about my dad, Laura came over with my food.

"Nan, what are you doing?" she said, turning to her great-grandmother.

"Just chatting with your friend, Colden. She seems like a very nice girl." Lillian motioned for Laura to lean down and she whispered something in her ear that made Laura's face go red. Oh, what I wouldn't give to know what she'd said. Laura stood up and then stumbled away as Lillian cackled.

"You young things don't know how much you're wasting," she said, standing up. I leapt up to help her, but she waved me off.

"What do you mean?" I asked.

"Hopefully you figure it out before you get too old. Come on, Minnie." She patted her leg and Minnie popped out from under the table and ran in circles around Lillian's feet. I hoped the pig wouldn't trip her, but she moseyed on back over to her table and I looked down at my food. Time to enjoy it and then get the fuck out of here.

I SAW with surprise someone had cleaned my car off when I dragged some of my luggage back out to throw it in the trunk. They'd even scraped the windshield. I wondered who had done that, because I definitely needed to thank them.

I went back to the front desk to talk to Michelle and tell her I was leaving.

"Thanks so much for the room and for everything. I really should have fought harder to pay, but I'm a little bit broke, so just tell everyone thank you, again. From the bottom of my cold and rotted heart."

That made her laugh.

"Are you sure you don't want to stay a little bit longer? We've got the room. And you're new and shiny and from the city. Tell me about the city." She put her elbows on the desk and leaned her chin into her hands while sighing wistfully.

"It's not that great," I said.

"It has to be better than here." This place didn't seem so bad, but I'd been here for less than two days. I could imagine it could get pretty monotonous after a while. And seeing the same people all the time and having to make small talk with them? Kill me now.

"Well, uh, thank you and I'm going to get on the road. Long drive."

"It was really nice to meet you. You should come back sometime."

"You could always visit me in Boston," I suggested.

"Someday," Michelle said with another sigh. I waved goodbye to her and looked around for Minnie, but didn't see the pig running around and didn't hear her. I also didn't see or say goodbye to Laura for obvious reasons. I wasn't going to see her until after Christmas and that was fine with me.

It was a relief to get in my car and fire up the GPS in my

phone to take me away. Until I turned the key and nothing happened.

"Fucking fuck," I said, trying again. Nada.

I sat there for a second and thought about laughing or crying or doing both at the same time, but I didn't. I tried the car one more time and then went back into the inn.

"Uh, so my car won't start?" I said to Michelle, who'd been scrolling something on her computer.

"Oh no, that's awful. Do you have AAA?"

"That would be no." I'd always thought about getting it, but never had. Now I was kicking myself.

"Listen, I bet someone here has jumper cables and could help. I might even have some in my trunk." Michelle put on her coat and we went back to out to my car and for the next half hour, she tried to jump my car. We'd get it started and then it would run for a few moments and then die. The check engine light came on and I was beginning to think there was something else wrong with it other than the battery.

"Well, fuck," I said, taking the keys out. I looked at Michelle and shrugged.

"Thanks for trying."

"You can call the local tow company. They might be able to take it somewhere to work on it. The closest place is Dave's, but he's on vacation for the next two weeks, so you might have to get it towed to town." Now I was ready to scream.

I shut the door of the car and wondered how long it would take to walk back to Boston.

"Come on inside and take a minute to get warm and come up with a plan." Michelle ushered me back inside and put me in a chair by the fireplace.

A few moments later, a cup of tea was pushed into my hands and then I was looking into the face of Laina.

"Michelle told me about your car trouble. Listen, how about you stay another night here and we can see about getting your car to town to get it fixed." I was suddenly incredibly tired. "Your room is still available. Why don't you go up and rest for a little while?"

I just nodded and let her take me upstairs and shove me back in the room.

"We'll bring your luggage up right away."

Whatever. I went into the bedroom and flopped facedown on the bed. I rolled onto my back and looked up at the ceiling. It had crown molding and beautiful tiles. They'd really made this place gorgeous.

There was a knock at the door and then someone let themselves in. I rolled off the bed and stumbled into the main room.

"Oh, hey," I said as Laura rolled my suitcases into the room.

"Can you just make a decision about staying or going and stick with it, so I don't have to do this again?" She panted a little, putting her hands on her hips.

"I didn't mess up my car on purpose," I said. "What happened to the other guy who moved my bags?" Laura rolled her eyes.

"That would be my useless cousin, Griffin, who always seems to disappear when any work needs to be done. He's probably smoking weed in the barn right now." That sounded about right.

"I'm sorry," I said, even though I wasn't sure why I was apologizing.

"It's fine. It's fine. So, you're staying again?"

"Looks like it. I'm just . . . I'm so fucking tired." I didn't mean to say that to her. I didn't like showing any kind of vulnerability with Laura. I was afraid she was going to use it against me, not that she ever really had. Mostly because I was never vulnerable in front of her.

She stood there for a second, as if she didn't know what to say.

"Sorry," I said again, and cringed. I didn't like all this apologizing. It was annoying.

"It's fine," she said again. "I just didn't expect to see you here." I mean, same.

"This is a beautiful place. Has your family always owned it?"

"Yup. Six generations."

"Your great-grandmother is hilarious." I was not doing great at making small talk with her and I should probably cut it out.

"She is," Laura said, looking out the door as some people passed by in the hallway. "I have to get back to work. These rooms won't clean themselves." Shit, she had to clean rooms too? That sucked.

"Are you getting paid?" I asked, which was probably rude, but whatever.

"Not nearly enough," she said, closing the door behind her.

There was a knock at my door a few minutes later and I wanted to put the Do Not Disturb sign on the doorknob so I could have a mental breakdown in peace. I'd burst into tears the second Laura left. I was tired and stressed and just . . . everything was hitting me that I was totally and completely alone.

My initial plan to be cozy and only rely on myself was falling apart and I didn't know what to do. I'd been lonely before, but it was easier to be lonely when you were alone and not surrounded by people. Like pressing your face against a window. I hated it.

I opened the door and found Laina there.

"Just wanted to check on you. I went ahead and called a local guy who sometimes works on cars. He's a good guy, second cousin. He's around to see his family and he's going to come over and look at your car and make a diagnosis. Might take him a while to fix it, though, because he might need parts." I sniffed and hoped she didn't see my red eyes.

"Thank you," I said, and Laina came into the room.

"Do you need a hug?" she asked, and the request was both so weird, and so welcome, that I just nodded and she enfolded me into her arms.

I couldn't remember the last time someone had hugged me. It might have been at my father's funeral three years ago. What an utterly depressing realization.

"It's okay, we'll get it sorted out," Laina said, as I breathed in her perfume.

"Thank you," I said and sniffed, trying not to get snot on her beautiful designer blazer. I pulled back and she reached for a tissue that was hidden in a porcelain box that had a painting of a ship on it.

"You're welcome to stay here with us, always. I know there is a little tension between you and Laura, but don't let that run you away. You can stay as long as you want, no charge."

I tried to protest, but she put her hand up.

"It's not charity. If you want to do something, we always need help with laundry and folding napkins and carrying bags and vacuuming carpets. We always need extra hands to help around here." I could imagine. Just the cleaning alone must be a time-consuming job.

"I can fold napkins," I said, blowing my nose quietly.

"Great. How about you meet me in the dining room in fifteen minutes and we'll go over some things."

She squeezed my shoulder with her hand and gave me a motherly look. At least I thought it was a motherly look. I hadn't really seen one in a long time, if my mother had ever looked at me like that. She'd left when I was so young that all my memories of her were hazy. I'm sure there were pictures somewhere, but I didn't want to look at them.

Laina left me again and I went to the bathroom to wash my face and get myself together before I went downstairs.

LAINA TOOK me into the laundry room in the back where there was a long table for folding various items like towels and napkins and so forth.

"This is Gen, my niece, and her brother Griffin is around here somewhere."

Gen looked to be about thirteen and was diligently folding napkins, her tongue between her teeth.

"Hi, Gen," I said with a little wave. She didn't look up.

Laina tapped her on the shoulder and she looked up. That was when I noticed the earbuds. Gen pulled them out and smiled.

"Hi," she said.

"Gen, this is Colden, and she's going to help you fold. Is that okay?" Gen nodded and then went back to her meticulous folding.

"Gen is autistic, and she might need to stim, just so you know." I blinked at Laina.

"She needs to flap her hands sometimes, or move her body. Okay?"

"Got it," I said.

Laina sat me in a chair across the table from Gen and put a stack of white napkins in front of me.

"We put them through the ironing machine and then fold them. I can teach you how to use that if you end up staying for a while." I could tell that she was trying to convince me, but I was still on the fence. I wanted to see what was up with my car before I made any other decisions.

Laina showed me how to fold the napkins and made sure I

could do it a few times without help to her standards before taking a call and saying she would check on me later.

It was pretty quiet in the laundry room, with the exception of the constantly grinding of the washers. One of the washers finished its cycle and a few moments later Laura walked in.

"What are you doing?" she asked.

"Working for my keep," I said. I didn't think I'd done a bad job with the folding. I had a nice stack of napkins going.

"You're working?" She didn't seem to be able to process me in the laundry room. She walked over to the washer and pulled a load of sheets out and threw them in the dryer before turning it on.

"Yeah, I didn't want to feel like I was mooching, or getting something for free. Your mom told me I could help."

Laura shook her head and sighed.

"I can't believe her. Okay, fine. Whatever." She left the room and I went back to folding. Laura's hostility toward me seemed to be growing by the hour and I wondered what would happen when she exploded. Hopefully I'd be on my way out before that happened.

Michelle came back to the laundry room and told me that Craig had looked at my car and wanted to talk to me. Great. I left the napkin folding and walked out to the lobby of the inn.

Craig looked just how I expected a man from Maine to look: flannel and a fisherman's knit hat.

"Hi, Craig, I'm Colden," I said, shaking his hand.

"Nice to meet you. So, I would need to get it on the lift, but I think you've got a couple of problems, in addition to needing a new battery."

My stomach dropped to my feet.

"I need a new battery?" I said. I didn't know how much that was going to cost me.

"Yeah, definitely at least that. I can drive to a parts supplier and get one for you, but that might not fix everything. I can tow it today and get a look at it. I've got a buddy that has a garage that will let me use his lift and tools. I can't take it until tomorrow, though." I wanted to cry again, but seriously, this guy was already going out of his way to help me.

"How much is this going to cost?"

Craig shuffled his feet and cleared his throat.

"How about you don't worry about that right now?" How could I not worry about it? Just the parts alone were going to be expensive, and then there was the labor? Fucking hell.

"Listen, it might be fine. I just need to check it. Don't panic before we know all the answers." There was something about his voice that steadied me. He seemed like a good guy, like Laina said.

"Okay," I said, because what else was I going to do? I wasn't good at any of this stuff. I didn't know what to do. I was just going to have to trust him.

Laina appeared at my shoulder and I turned to her.

"Hi Craig, thank you so much for coming," Laina said, and I wanted to cry again, but I wasn't going to let myself. I'd already cried too much at this place. Too much meant at all. I didn't like crying in front of anyone, because then they'd try to take care of you and that was just the worst. I just wanted people to leave me alone. That hug I'd shared with Laina earlier had been a fluke and I wasn't going to let it happen again. I blamed all the holiday cheer for weakening my defenses. I needed to freeze my heart up again.

"No problem. I'm just going to come back and tow the car tomorrow and once I get it on the lift, I can let you all know what's going on in there." He gave me a smile, but it wasn't reassuring. This was going to cost me, I knew it.

Laina pulled Craig aside and they talked in hushed tones. Like I wasn't even there. Craig looked back at me and then to Laina and nodded.

"I'll get back to you tomorrow," Craig said to me and then shared some more words with Laina before exiting.

"I'm so sorry about your car, but I'm not sorry that you'll be staying with us for a little longer. It's almost lunch, are you hungry?" I was and I let her lead me into the dining room and put me in a seat. There were a few people sitting at tables and drinking coffee and even a few people playing board games. I didn't even remember the last time I'd played a board game. Probably with Dad.

I stopped that train of thought before it could pull out of the station and looked out the window instead. The snow sparkled in the sun like diamonds. A few people were outside near the gazebo, walking and pausing to throw snowballs at each other. One of them kind of looked like Griffin, the slacker.

"Hi, are you Colden?" a voice asked, and I looked up.

"Yes?" I said, wondering who this was and how they knew my name.

"Hi, sorry, I'm Greta Brown. I'm Laura's cousin." Yup, there was that resemblance again. Like they'll all been made at the same beautiful factory.

"Hi," I said. Was I going to be subjected to meeting the entire Sterling family?

"I just wanted to introduce myself. You met my daughter, Gen, and my son, Griffin." These people had a thing with names all starting with the same letter, didn't they?

"Oh, yeah. They seem like great kids," I said, because that was a thing you were supposed to say to people about their kids, right?

"We're playing Scrabble over here, would you like to join us?" No, I definitely did not.

"I'm okay," I said. I wanted Laina to come back and bring me some napkins to fold so people would stop coming up to me.

"Just thought I would ask. There's also books in the den, if you're interested." My books were upstairs. I had to stop leaving my room without a book in my hand. That was just asking for disaster.

"What kind of books?" I asked, and then I was getting up and walking toward the books, as if drawn there by a spell. I couldn't help it.

"So fiction is here, non-fic is over there," she said. The books were on shelves and in hutches and pilled on surfaces and just . . . everywhere. It was meant to look haphazard, but I had the feeling everything had been carefully arranged. Bowls of pinecones and berries sat atop huge art volumes and holly decorated the tops of all the hutches and bookshelves. I looked up and saw mistletoe hanging from both of the chandeliers in the room. Uh oh. Definitely gonna avoid that shit.

There was someone sitting and reading in front of the fireplace, and I didn't need to see anything other than the hair draped across the back of the wing chair to know who it was.

"Hey, what are you doing in here?" Greta said, walking in front of the chair to talk to Laura.

"Taking a break," Laura said. I heard her close her book and get out of the chair. I tried to see the title of the book, but couldn't. Our eyes locked and it became hard to breathe. I didn't know what to say or do, so I just kind of wobbled on my feet until Greta cleared her throat and asked me if I wanted some tea.

"Sure," I said, and she left the room in a rush, leaving me and Laura alone. Why weren't there more people in here? Objectively, this was the best room in the inn.

Bing Crosby played softly from a turntable as the fire crackled.

"You must go through a lot of firewood," I said. There were so many damn fireplaces here and they were always lit, as far as I'd seen.

"We do. I have to haul it in nearly every day," she said. She'd changed from her work outfit and had on sweater that was probably cashmere and black pants with leopard-print ballet flats. Did she ever look casual?

"Are you off the clock?"

"For a few hours. I'll be back on for dinner. We're short some of our regular help, so here I am."

"It sucks that you can't relax on your vacation." Sure, she was a pain in my ass, but the one thing I could say for her was that she worked hard. We both did. I just hoped I worked a little bit harder and got a promotion. I couldn't afford not to.

"It's fine," she said, fiddling with the spine of the book.

"What are you reading?" Books were my comfort zone. I could talk to just about anyone about books.

"Sense and Sensibility," she said, holding the hardcover up.

"Good choice," I said, nodding.

"I didn't ask for your approval," she snapped. Yikes. She turned away from me and sat back down in the chair. I wasn't sure what to do, but I found my feet carrying me over to the fireplace and into the chair that was next to hers.

"I'm so fucking tired," she said, rubbing her face with her hands. I'd said the same thing not that long ago.

"At least your car isn't fucked up and you didn't rent an imaginary cottage like I did." I wasn't going to live that one down. I was going to be ancient and still remember this whole thing with embarrassment. Not one of my finer moments.

Greta arrived with an actual tea tray. With a sugar bowl and everything.

"Here we are. I also brought some cookies in case you wanted a little something." It was nearly lunchtime, but I wasn't going to say no to a cookie.

"Thank you," I said, picking up a little gingerbread cookie that was decorated with white frosting.

"Thanks, Greta," Laura said, and there was an edge to her

voice. The cousins shared a look that I couldn't interpret and then Greta left again.

"What was that about?"

"Nothing," Laura said, glaring into her teacup as if it had offended her.

Laura and I sat in silence as I munched on a cookie and she sipped her tea. It was tense, and I wanted to run away. I was saved from having to do that with the arrival of Minnie.

"Hello, piggy. Can she have cookies?" I asked. I had no idea what pigs could and couldn't eat. I'd never had a pet before, other than a goldfish that died a week after I won it at a carnival and for which my dad had given a grand funeral, even pulling out his old trumpet to play "Taps" as we flushed it.

"She can have pretty much anything." Minnie put her chin on my knee and made this cute little snuffling noise and wagged her tail back and forth. There was a tiny little bow on it. How cute.

"Here you go, Minnie," I said, holding a cookie out for her. She took it delicately from my fingers and crunched it.

"How did your great-grandmother end up with a huge pig?" Laura snorted and I stared at her. She shook her head and I saw a little break in her armor.

"She meant to buy a teacup pig. She ordered her online and then made my mom take her to the airport to pick Minnie up. She was tiny for a few weeks, but then she started growing and growing and we realized she'd been scammed, but by then it was too late and Nan loved her, so she stayed." That was so cute.

"I can't believe she spent five thousand dollars on a pig." I stared at her, my mouth open.

"Holy shit."

"Yeah. But it's her money, she can spend it how she wants. Whether that's on scam pigs or vintage gowns or books or anything else." I was guessing Lillian had a lot of money. This whole family seemed to. I wanted to get to the root of that, but you couldn't really come out and say "hey, where is your generational wealth from?"

"Goals," I said, about Lillian.

"She is." Laura let a soft smile cross her face and I realized that I rarely saw her smile. Granted, I rarely looked at her for longer than a few seconds or acknowledged her presence. I tried to keep my head down and my eyes on the prize at the office.

Minnie scampered off and I was left alone with Laura again, so I got up and started browsing the shelves. There was quite a collection, including an entire hutch full of romance. Our agency did all kinds of books, but the agent Laura and I assisted for did mostly adult romance, young adult books, and selective non-fiction. It was a good variety, so we got to see all kinds of submissions.

I pulled a recent romance that I actually had a copy of in my suitcase upstairs and sat back down to read. I could feel Laura watching me for a few moments, but then she went back to reading her own book.

My body sunk into the chair and I pulled my feet up, kicking off my shoes. In between bites of delicious cookies and sips of tea, I let myself fall into the book and everything else around me fell away. I even forgot about Laura until she coughed and got up to put a different record on.

"It's time for lunch," Greta said, pausing in the entryway between the den and the dining room. "Come sit with us, Colden." I wanted to protest, but Laura was glaring at me and I found myself agreeing, just to annoy her.

"Great," Greta said, and I followed her into the dining room.

They'd pushed several tables together, and I found myself sitting next to Laura, with Greta on my other side. Her husband, Hank was next to her. He beamed at me and said hello, and then everyone else at the table introduced themselves. I was never going to remember anyone's name, but I tried to put a face and a name together in my mind. There were aunts and uncles and cousins and grandparents.

"How much of your family is here?" I asked Laura, as the menus were passed around.

"A lot," she said. I'd hazard a guess that half the town had the last name of Sterling, or was related to someone who did. I shuddered and it brought me back to my own small-town upbringing. I'd hated it.

This time Laura didn't wait on me, but it was Michelle, who'd traded out her front-desk attire for the waitress uniform.

Laura ordered the winter vegetable salad with grilled chicken and I got the same. Once we'd all gotten through our orders, it was back to having nearly every single set of eyes on me. That was pretty intimidating.

"Are you going to stay for Christmas?" Hank asked. "You can help us find the pickle." Laura sighed heavily beside me.

"I'm sorry, the what?"

"The Christmas pickle," Hank said, and Greta smiled at him in the way that people who were in love smiled at the object of their affection.

"And what would that be?" I asked. Surely this wasn't going to turn into a dirty story? There were children around.

"Every year someone hides the Christmas pickle ornament on one of the trees on Christmas Eve, and everyone gets a chance to look for it. If you find it, you get to open one present before you go to sleep, and then you get to be the pickle hider for the next year. I'm the pickle hider this year." He seemed really jazzed about this pickle thing and that was pretty charming to see a middle-aged man excited about something so silly.

"Do you have any traditions?" he asked, and I felt Greta nudge him.

"Uh, not really." I didn't want to talk about celebrating Christmas anymore.

Greta hissed something in Hank's ear, and his face went a little red.

I was saved from answering by the arrival of drinks and then Laina started a conversation about the weather that got everyone really animated for some reason.

"Are you still she today?" Laura said in my ear, leaning close. A light scent hit my nose, but I couldn't put my finger on it. I knew I'd smelled it before, and I realized it must be Laura's perfume.

"Yes, I'm still she," I said. "Do, um, have you told them? About me?" Most of the time I just let people think I was a cis woman because it was easier than explaining what being nonbinary was to someone who thought there were only two genders.

"Yes, they know. Michelle is queer too, Mel and Sue are married, Judy and Susan are married, Uncle Dan is trans, and then there's me. This is a very queer family. Nan gives out free hugs at Pride every year." Wow. I had no idea. I looked around the table and saw nothing but kindness radiating back at me. How unexpected.

I relaxed a little more and chatted with Greta and Hank, and Griffin wandered in to get some food and then wandered away again. There was a small group of surly teens he seemed to be a part of that used the inn as their hangout place until Laina sent them outside to shovel the parking lot or to get more wood for the fires.

The food was still incredible and the talk at the table was nice. I didn't feel the need to participate, I could just sit back and be involved, but not have to speak.

Laura was tense beside me the whole time, and I wanted to tell her to calm the fuck down because it was getting annoying. What was her deal?

After lunch, I decided I wanted to get outside, even though it was freezing. I went and got my coat, put on my books, and covered up nearly every bit of exposed skin before going back down to the lobby.

"Where are you going?" Laura asked. She'd been leaning on the counter and talking to Michelle.

"To the beach," I said, my voice muffled by the scarf covering my mouth.

"It's freezing out," Laura said.

"Thanks for pointing that out, I had no idea," I said, gesturing to my outfit.

"You're going to get lost," she said.

"No, I'm not. The ocean is right there," I said, pointing toward the front door. Laura closed her eyes as if she was losing her patience.

"Give me ten minutes." She headed for the stairs.

"Where are you going?" I asked.

"I'm going to grab my boots and my coat and I'm going with you. With your luck you'll get eaten by a bear or slip on the ice and fall into the ocean and drown."

"I'm not *that* helpless," I said. "I have been near the ocean before without incident." I wasn't going to tell her about that one time my dad had to rescue me.

Laura ignored me and continued up the stairs.

"Do you want to come? Now I'm afraid she's going to push me in the ocean," I said to Michelle.

"I wish I could, but I have to watch the desk." Great, it was going to be just me and Laura.

She came back downstairs in a puffy coat with a fur-lined hood (hopefully fake) and boots.

"Come on," she said, putting the hood up in dramatic fashion before heading for the front door. I thought about bolting upstairs and locking the door and staying in for the rest of the day, but I really needed some sunshine on my face, even if it was really cold out.

"Oh, shit it's cold," was the first thing I said as the inn door shut behind us.

"Told you," Laura said.

Chapter Three

"COME ON," Laura said, walking carefully up the driveway. It was icy in places, so I stepped as gingerly as I could so I didn't have all my weight in one foot.

"You look ridiculous," Laura said as I picked my way to the shoveled path that wasn't covered in ice.

"Shut up, at least I didn't fall."

Laura kept walking and I stayed behind her until we crossed the road and headed toward the beach. The wind whipped at the strands of hair that had escaped from under my hat.

The beach was deserted and mostly covered in snow. Piles upon piles of seaweed had built up and crunched loudly as we stepped over them. I nearly tripped on a piece of driftwood and grabbed for Laura to steady myself.

"Sorry," I said, but she was silent.

The waves lapped at the sand as we walked and tried to stay warm.

"Why did you want to come out here?" Laura said.

"I don't know, it seemed like a good idea at the time," I said, wrapping my arms around myself. In spite of my thick coat, the ocean wind whipped through the nooks and crannies and chilled me to the bone.

"Sometimes I come out here and walk," she said, looking out at the water that was the color of iron. Unforgiving and cold as hell.

"Do you come back here for every holiday?"

"Yeah. I'm kind of obligated." Her breath looked like smoke in the air.

"Do you like anything about it?" She hadn't seemed to, but maybe that was just because she didn't like me.

"Oh, I love visiting, but I wouldn't want to move back. I'm pretty much one of the only people who've left town. I think my mom had a mental breakdown when I announced I was leaving for college and probably not coming back. I think she tries to lure me to come work with her, but it's not going to work. I'm not living here." That was exactly how I felt about my own hometown. So many people were born there, lived there, and then died there, and never ventured anywhere else. If that worked for them, great, but expecting everyone to feel the same way as they did was a constant annoyance to me.

"Your family seems great."

"That's because they're not your family." I laughed.

"Fair enough." We covered the length of the beach and reached the edge that was studded with rocks that were covered in snow.

"Another lap?" she asked, and I nodded. My entire body was pretty much numb now, so the cold wasn't bothering me anymore.

"You don't have family to spend Christmas with?" she asked. "Sorry, that sounded accusatory. I didn't mean it that way."

I didn't really want to talk about this, but the cold must have loosened my tongue.

"Not really, no." As little as I knew about her history, she didn't know anything about me because I did my best not to share anything that was even remotely personal.

"I'm sorry," she said. "That must be hard."

I made a non-committal sound.

"I'm sorry I'm such a bitch right now. I just . . . all I wanted was to have a break from my family trying to get me to come back here and just being around them is a lot. Plus, I get roped into helping because 'that's what family does' and I just get tired." I could understand that.

"And then having me here probably didn't help."

She looked over at me.

"No, not really."

I thought back to the first day we'd met, when I'd walked into the office and been introduced to her.

"Hi," she said, shaking my hand. My initial impression was that she was beautiful and cold, but I chalked that up to being nervous too. We had a meeting-slash-orientation with our new boss, Ping, who went over our job descriptions and set expectations for what we'd be doing.

I'd started out doing an internship at another publishing house, but Laura had started here, so she already had a leg up on me and that was beyond irritating when she seemed to have a rapport with everyone, even though it was her first day as a paid employee. The real problems started when Ping assigned projects and she jumped in and tried to take every single one, told me what I should be doing, and just . . . took over. I'd never seen someone so aggressive about anything, and it was an adjustment. My nerves got the better of me and I was flustered the whole day, making little mistakes and not the best first impression. I also spilled coffee all over my brand-new tan pants and had to wear them like that the rest of the day.

Her confidence in what she said and her ideas was like sandpaper against my skin. What the hell did she know? Who *was* she? I couldn't figure her out.

In the year since we'd started working together, my conflict with her had just grown. I swear she searched through the submissions box at all hours of the night to nab the most promising ones that she could read and then send to Ping. I had no proof, but when we met to discuss who would read what, I almost always got the crappy ones that went right in the trash. It was like a race with her, and I was up for it, but she'd still managed to get the jump on me enough times.

She also kissed Ping's ass something terrible. It was so fucking obvious.

"What happened to your family, if you don't mind me asking?" she said, bringing me back to the present moment and the ice-cold beach.

"I do mind," I snapped, and then took a bracing breath. "My dad is dead and my mom is gone and they were both only children and my grandparents are dead. There. Happy now?" People always wanted to know until you told them and afterward they realized they didn't want to know and the conversation basically died of natural causes.

"I'm so sorry," she said, and our eyes locked again. Her cheeks were bright red from the wind and the cold, as well as her lips. I'd never noticed how pretty they were before. I mean, everything about her was pretty, but I'd always seen the whole package, and not individual features.

She sniffed and I pulled a tissue from my pocket.

"Here," I said, giving it to her.

"Thanks."

"So you spend holidays alone?"

"Yes," I said, getting exasperated.

"I didn't know that," she said, stopping and staring out at the waves again. The wind whipped little white caps on each wave, making them look like they were frosted for a moment.

"Let's go back," I said. I couldn't feel any part of my body anymore, and thinking was starting to get more difficult.

"Okay," she said, and we headed back to the inn. The second I came into the warmth, I wanted to cry because it almost hurt.

"I'm a human popsicle. A humansicle," I told Michelle as I tried to get my gloves off with frozen fingers.

"Do you need some help?" she asked, coming around the desk and helping me pull off the gloves. We both laughed when they got stuck and I had to yank and almost hit myself in the face.

"What are you doing?" Laura asked, coming up behind us and stomping her boots off on the front rug.

"Nothing," I said, trying to grip the zipper of my coat and failing.

"Here," Michelle said, grabbing it for me and pulling it down.

"Thanks," I said. My fingers and toes and face were pins and needles and I shivered and pulled the coat off.

"You should sit by the fire and thaw out," Michelle said, taking my coat and hanging it up as I pulled my hat off.

"Good idea." All I wanted to do right now was sit by the fire in the den and read some more of that book with a cup of hot chocolate and hope no one talked to me.

I stood up from getting my boots off to find Laura giving me a strange look.

"What?" I wondered if I had something on my face, or if my nose was running or something.

"Nothing," she said, looking away and pressing her lips together. "Nothing."

Okay?

Leaving her in the lobby, I headed for the den. Unfortunately, there were several other people in there already, including Lillian, Minnie, and two of Laura's aunts who I was pretty sure were married.

Damn.

Everyone greeted me with smiles and I wanted to run away. I didn't like this kind of attention.

"We're going to have afternoon tea, would you like to join us?" Lillian asked. "There are fresh scones in the kitchen." I could go up to my room and be alone, or I could suck it up and get tea and scones with the nice people.

"Absolutely," I said. I couldn't turn down a scone.

"You want to have a scone, Laura?" Lillian asked and I turned to find Laura with a brooding look on her face. Even that was gorgeous. Did she ever look ugly? Could she? I didn't think so.

"Sure," she said, but she didn't look as if she relished the idea. What was up with her? She'd been fine when we'd been on the beach a few moments ago and now it was like a cloud hung over her head. Weird.

Someone moved the furniture around so we could sit in a little circle to have tea. Michelle went and fetched a few tea trays with a variety of tea, honey ("from our own bees," she said), and scones with jam and clotted cream.

"If that doesn't look like heaven, I don't know what does," Lillian said, making a plate for herself and then a second plate that she placed in front of Minnie.

"Nan," Laura warned, but Lillian ignored her and petted Minnie.

"Let an old woman have her fun," she said, and Laura looked into her cup.

"Are you ready for activities tonight?" one of the aunts asked.

"Activities?" I said warily. I didn't like the sound of that.

"Yes, every year we have activities for the nights before Christmas. Tonight we're decorating cookies. You're welcome to join us. Tomorrow night we're making wreaths to put on graves at the cemetery, and then Tuesday night it's Christmas Charades." I knew I was supposed to be excited about all of those prospects, but I'd rather eat glass than play Christmas Charades. I'd rather eat glass, walk on glass, and be stabbed by glass all at the same time.

Laura elbowed me and I glared at her. What? Like I had to participate?

Everyone was staring at me in expectation.

"Well, I don't know how long I'm going to be here. Decorating cookies could be fun?" It sounded like a question.

"It will be," Lillian said with a wink.

I was going to do whatever I could to not be here the night they did Christmas Charades. There was no way in hell I would participate in that. No matter what.

We enjoyed our tea and scones, but I couldn't stop looking at Laura. She had her gloomy on and I almost asked her if everything was okay before I reminded myself that I didn't care. No, I definitely didn't care.

I decided I needed to take a shower and maybe have some alone time for a while, so I headed back to my room, but found Laura following me.

"What are you doing?" I asked. She opened a closet near my room and pulled something out.

"Bringing you fresh towels," she said.

"Oh, you don't have to. I've got plenty." She ignored me and followed me into the room and put the towels in the bathroom, taking the "dirty" ones with her to be washed, probably by her.

"Thank you?" I said and she opened her mouth as if she was going to say something, but then snapped it closed.

"You okay?" I asked.

"Fine," she said, but that was definitely a lie. She huffed away and shut the door loudly behind her. What the hell?

I shook my head and went for the shower, stripping off my shirt and bra and I almost screamed when the door opened again.

"What the fuck?" I said, covering myself.

"Did you want a robe?" Laura asked, her eyes wide as she held one out. She was staring and I turned my back.

"No, go away!"

Laura dropped the robe and backed out of the room as I ran to the bathroom, my hands holding my boobs. I shut and locked the bathroom door behind me and put my hand on my racing heart.

Laura had just seen me shirtless. I mean, I didn't think she'd really seen anything since I'd covered myself so fast, but she might have gotten a glimpse of my tits. This day was just getting better and better.

∽

I DIDN'T WANT to go back downstairs after my shower and reading time, but I was also hungry and didn't want to make a big deal out of Laura seeing me. It wasn't a big deal. She had boobs, I had boobs, they were pretty much the same. At least that's what I told myself as I walked down the stairs and tried to sneak into the dining room without seeing anyone.

Of course that wasn't what happened.

Minnie ran up to me and then Lillian said hello and then Hank did and then everyone else did. They'd pushed the tables together again and this time they'd even saved me a seat.

I tried to be sneaky about looking around for Laura, but I didn't see her. Someone was playing on the piano again, a crisp, sweet melody that I knew, but couldn't place.

I glanced over and saw a sleek ponytail that I could have placed anywhere.

"Is that Laura?" I asked and Greta looked toward the piano.

"Oh, yes. She grew up playing. We all thought she might go to school for music, but she decided on publishing instead."

Greta said the word "publishing" like it tasted bad in her mouth. What was wrong with publishing?

Laura wasn't just a person who had taken a few lessons and could plunk out a tune or two. No, she was a real professional and I had to admit that I was impressed as she finished one song with a flourish and launched right into the next without pause.

I was completely distracted by Laura and didn't notice Michelle trying to take my drink order. I'd even forgotten about the fact that she'd seen me without a shirt earlier and I should be completely embarrassed.

"Sorry," I said, "What was that?"

"Do you want the drink special? We have mulled wine." Honestly, that sounded perfect, so I ordered a glass and then she told me the specials. They went in one ear and out the other. Laura on the piano was completely mesmerizing. I could only see her back but there was passion written all over her body as she threw herself into playing. The music brought tears to my eyes and chills to my skin. As if she'd bewitched me with her music.

I found myself getting up from my chair and walking over to the piano, as if in a trance.

I walked around so I could see her face and it was . . . magic. Pure magic. Her eyes were closed and the emotion written on her face was something that I had never seen before. She was lost to another world that I could never hope to touch. I stood there and realized, probably too late, that it was a little creepy, so I moved to go back to the table and tripped over a decorative tree that fell over with a crash. Laura's eyes snapped open and she stared at me and then down at the plant and back as if she didn't know what was happening.

"I'm sorry," I said, gesturing at the plant and the soil that had spilled all over the floor. I opened and closed my hands, as if that would fix everything.

Laura got up from the piano and walked away as I crouched by the tree.

"Help?" I said under my breath. Laura came back a few moments later with a dustpan, a brush, and some cleaning wipes.

"I've got it," she said, her voice sharp as I tried to clean.

"No, I did it, I should clean it," I said, taking the brush and dustpan out of her hands. "This is my mess." I could feel her protesting, but she just let me sweep up the soil as she put the plant upright again and then I used the wipes to get rid of the last of the soil.

"You play really well," I said, as I held out the supplies. That was when I noticed what she was wearing and my brain stopped working.

She wore a black suit with white ruffled shirt underneath and a black thin tie. Laura always looked gorgeous, but this was next level. She'd even done a smoky eye that made her already-gorgeous eyes look deep and mysterious.

"I'll take care of that," she said, taking the supplies from my hands. I didn't know what else to say, so I stood there until she came back.

"I'm going to go back to playing. I think your drinks are here and everyone else is ordering. You should go sit down." I wanted to say something, but I couldn't find the right words, so I left her, heading back to the table.

I spent the rest of the evening trying not to stare at Laura as she played. She took a break to eat, but she wasn't sitting anywhere near me. I kept losing the threads of conversation and kept having to ask people to repeat themselves. I was a complete distracted mess. The more I tried not to think of her, the more I thought about her.

"You feeling okay, darling?" Lillian said, coming over to sit next to me as a few people left the dining room and the empty plates were collected by Michelle and a disgruntled Griffin.

"I'm fine," I said, and the room was suddenly quiet as Laura stopped playing.

"Are you sure? You seem a million miles away." I wasn't miles away. Just a few feet.

"I'm fine," I repeated, and she put her hand on my shoulder and looked into my eyes.

"Anything you want to tell me?" She asked.

"No. I don't think so." I didn't know what was going on with me. It was as if I was in a dream, or an alternate reality. I looked down at my hands to reassure myself that they were mine.

"You just let me know. I've got two ears and many years of experience. I've been married eight times." The last part she whispered, and I stared at her, shocked.

"Eight?" I asked. I'd never heard of someone other than Elizabeth Taylor being married that many times.

She beamed and nodded as if she was pretty proud of that number.

"I liked being married, but I got bored easily." Oh, well, I guess that made sense. "I also look ravishing in white."

I started laughing and she joined in. I officially adored her.

"What's going on over here?" Laura's voice cut through my laughter and I looked up at her and it was like staring into the bright sun. I wanted to shade my eyes.

"I was just telling Colden about my husbands."

"Nan, no one wants to hear about that, gross," Laura said.

"I want to hear about them. Which one was your favorite?" I turned back to Lillian and she grinned and thought for a second.

"That's a tie between William and Thatcher. William was better in bed, but Thatcher had the most gorgeous house in California." I burst out laughing and Laura made a disgusted noise and covered her ears.

"Oh my god, Nan! You can't say things like that!" Lillian ignored her.

"It all depends on what you want and what you need. Don't forget about either of those, and you'll do well. The other thing to remember is that people change and the person that's right for you now might not be right for the you that you'll be in ten years. Doesn't mean the relationship was a failure. Good things can last a short time and still be good." I wanted this woman to write an advice book for me.

"Nan, you have to stop," Laura begged, her face completely red.

"Fine, fine. That's enough advice for tonight. Now how about you help your Nan get to the den. My bones are stiff tonight." She held out her hand and Laura helped her up. Minnie dashed over, and I saw that she had a jingling collar around her neck. Like a dog.

"Hey, are you going to stick around for cookie decorating?" Michelle asked, as I watched Laura lead Lillian into the den and get her seated in one of the chairs by the fire. Lillian grabbed Laura's ear and pulled it down to say something to her and then pat her cheek. I wanted to have a great grandmother. Something in my chest started to ache like it hadn't in a long time.

"What?" I said, looking up at Michelle.

"Are you going to decorate cookies with us? You can eat as much frosting as you want." She really seemed eager and I couldn't figure out why. Laura came back and looked at me and then Michelle.

"Are you going to decorate cookies?" Laura asked.

"Is that the question of the night? Why are you all so invested in me joining you? It's getting a little weird," I said, trying to joke.

"You don't have to, if you don't want to," Michelle said, but she was practically pouting. I looked at Laura and even she looked like she wanted me to say yes. I couldn't handle all this peer pressure.

"Okay, okay. But I'm not promising that they're going to look good. I'm no artist."

"Oh, that doesn't matter," Michelle said. "Let me get everything cleared up and then we can start."

Laura and I left the dining room and headed into the den.

"I have to put some more wood on the fire," she said, walking away from me. What was with everyone tonight?

My car was getting towed tomorrow and then I could hopefully get out of this place. I felt like the holiday cheer was affecting my brain.

A record played a variety of soft holiday songs in the background as I watched Laura tend the fire. Must be a lot of work to keep them all burning. I wondered why they didn't get the gas units that looked like real fires. Lot less work, but maybe it was the charm they were after. That would make sense.

"Okay, cookie time everyone," Michelle announced. Everyone seemed eager and we went back to the dining room to find trays and trays of cookies: sugar, gingerbread, spice, and others. Veritable towers of cookies and bags and bags of frosting in different colors already in piping bags. Then there were the bowls of toppings and sprinkles and colored sugars.

"There is so much sugar in this room," I said. My heart was racing thinking about it.

"Isn't it great?" Michelle said, touching my shoulder to step by me. I heard a disgusted sound behind me and glanced back to see Laura.

"What?" I said. Obviously, she'd made the noise for some reason.

"Nothing," she said, feigning innocence. "Let's decorate some cookies."

~

I WASN'T GOING to lie: Decorating cookies was a blast. I got frosting all over my fingers and everything I did looked like crap, but I came up with a system. Every cookie that I messed up ended up in my mouth so no one else could see how awful it was.

"Are you going to finish decorating one?" Laura asked as she put the finishing touches on a gorgeous Christmas tree with ornaments on it. All her cookies were ready to hang in the Louvre. Why was she so damn good at everything? It was constantly being shoved in my face.

"Yes," I said, grabbing a gingerbread cookie in the shape of a person. "Gonna make a nonbinary gingerbread person," I said. In the smallest writing I could manage, I wrote "she/they" on the person's chest and then gave her eyes and features and an outfit. It looked a mess when I was done, but I was happy with myself. I made a few more with different pronouns.

"Cute," Laura said, leaning over my shoulder and looking at my little group of gingerbread people.

"Thanks," I said. They weren't fine art, but they made me happy, so I guess that was what mattered.

"It's not a contest, you know. We tried that and there was actual bloodshed. It was an accident, but still." I could imagine this family being competitive. They seemed to be intense about everything.

"I know. Yours are too pretty to eat."

"Thank you, but that's not true." She picked up the cookie she'd just finished and shoved half of it in her mouth.

She ate the rest of the cookie and dabbed her mouth with a napkin.

"See?"

"Badass," I said, clapping for her.

"Shut up. Don't make fun of me or I'll squirt you." She held up the bag of frosting in one hand like a weapon.

I gasped.

"You wouldn't dare."

"Oh, I would. I *love* dares." I saw a devious sparkle in her eyes just before she squeezed the frosting bag and a stream of it hit me right in the face.

"You did not!" I picked up a bag and got her back and we both screamed as we emptied both bags on each other. She reached out and smeared my entire face and both laughed so hard that both of us were having trouble breathing. I could barely see. There was even frosting in my eyelashes.

"What is going on over here?" a voice asked, and I turned to see Laina.

"She did it," Laura and I said at the exact same time, pointing at each other.

Laina shook her head, but she was hiding a smile.

"Aren't you both adults?" she asked, as I blinked through the frosting. Laina handed me and Laura napkins to wipe ourselves off, but it was going to take something more than that. I needed a pressure hose to get this off.

I wiped my eyes so I could see and Laura giggled as she tried to clean her face.

"Come on," she said, taking my arm and leading me to the back and the employee bathroom. It was big enough to have a long sink that we stood at as she passed me a hand towel soaked in warm water.

"I'm a mess," she said, looking in the mirror.

I almost said that she was a beautiful mess, but I stopped myself just in time. I licked frosting from my lips and tried to get it out of my hair.

"I think I need a shower." That was the only way I was going to get clean.

"Same," she said, looking at me. For a moment, we stared at each other and then she slowly reached out and wiped some frosting from my nose and as if she wasn't aware that she was doing it, licked her finger.

I stopped breathing.

What was happening? I was in a bathroom with my work nemesis and all I could think about was the way she'd licked the frosting off her finger. It was like when she played the piano. I was caught in her spell again.

"We should go. Back," she said, her voice catching. I found myself leaning toward her. I couldn't help it. She inhaled sharply through her nose and threw the washcloth in the hamper near the door.

"I'll be there in a second," I said, but she was already gone. I looked at myself in the mirror.

"What the fuck?" I said to my reflection. She didn't answer back.

Chapter Four

I WENT BACK to my room soon after that because I couldn't deal with making small talk while there were so many thoughts running through my head. Nearly all of them centered on Laura.

How much had she seen earlier? I'd covered up quickly, but had she seen me? What did she think? Did she like what she had seen? What did she think about when she played the piano?

I got in the shower and scrubbed the frosting from my skin and hair. My clothes were a lost cause and I wondered if they'd let me do some laundry here before I left.

After my shower I tried to read, but it wasn't taking, no matter what book I tried. I couldn't stop thinking about Laura. Even though I'd eaten my weight in cookies, I was still hungry and considered getting room service, knowing who would probably deliver it.

I paced around the sitting area for almost a half an hour before I picked the phone and talked to Michelle.

"Hey, can I order some tea and some chips and salsa?"

They made fresh salsa on the premises from local tomatoes, peppers, and onions. I'd had some already and it was the shit.

"Yeah, sure. It'll be up in a few minutes."

I waited right by the door and listened for footsteps. At last there was a knock at the door, but when I opened it, I found Griffin instead of Laura.

"Oh," I said, unable to hide being disappointed.

"Room service," he said in a bored voice, shoving the tray at me.

"Thanks," I said, taking it from him. "I'm sorry, I don't have any more cash to give you." He huffed and shuffled down the hall toward the stairs without another word. Ah, to be young and surly.

I didn't know why I wanted to see Laura so much. I'd gone from being so glad I wasn't going to see her in two weeks to ordering something on the off chance she'd bring it to my room.

This was a serious problem.

I munched at my chips and salsa and almost scalded my mouth trying to drink my too-hot tea and flipped through the channels until I moved to the bed. Tomorrow my car would get towed and I'd find out if I could get out of this holiday hellhole or if I was going to be surrounded by the love and joy of the Sterlings.

~

"IT'S GOING to cost *how* much?" I screeched into the phone. "Sorry Craig."

"No, I'm sorry. I know it's a lot. I won't do anything unless you give me the green light." It wasn't even the amount. It was that I literally could not pay for it right now. Not until the refund for the imaginary cottage came in, which was taking its sweet time.

"Um, okay," I said, on the verge of tears. I'd been pacing my room since lunch, waiting for him to call. All I'd wanted was for him to tell me that it was going to be twenty bucks and the car was fine, but that wasn't what was happening. No, I'd been dealt yet another shitty hand, and I didn't have anyone to bail me out. Nope, I was on my own with this mess.

I closed my eyes and breathed for a second, and tried not to think about Dad, and what he would have said to me if he was here. That just made it worse.

Craig was still talking about car things, but it was going in one ear and out the other. All I'd heard was the insurmountable amount it would cost to fix my car.

"I'm going to have to think about this and call you back," I said, so I could get off the phone and cry in peace. He apologized again and hung up and I collapsed on one of the chairs in the little reading nook in my suite.

I couldn't stop myself from crying. Most of the time I was able to be strong, but when my plans had fallen apart, it was like I'd fallen apart and my normal ability to "keep calm and carry on" was shattered.

"What am I going to do?" I said, wiping the hot tears from my eyes and trying to keep from hyperventilating.

There was a knock at my door and I sniffed, trying to be quiet so whomever it was would go away. I waited a few moments and they knocked again.

"Colden?" a muffled voice said. "Are you in there?"

I didn't answer. I knew Laura's voice.

"You know I have a master key I can use if I want."

"Don't you dare!" I called out.

"I knew you were in there. Can I come in?"

"No." I didn't want her to see me like this. I was pretty proud of myself for never having cried at work in front of her. I wanted to keep that streak going. Her mom had seen me cry, but that was different.

"I'm going to unlock the door if you don't let me innnnn," she said, drawing the last word out.

"Oh my god, what is wrong with you?"

Laura had reached a whole new level of annoyance. I got up and swung the door open.

"What? Did you want to see me crying and looking like shit, because here you go. Might want to take a pic so you can share it with the internet." I wasn't feeling very nice at the moment.

Laura looked at me and that was when I noticed Minnie by her feet, wagging her little tail and looking up at me. I didn't know if pigs could smile, but it looked like Minnie was smiling at me and happy to see me. She skipped into the room and started snuffling around.

"She's obsessed with you," Laura said, following the pig into the room.

"Why don't you both come in?" I said, closing the door.

"Are you okay? Craig was talking to my mom and I overheard."

"Not really," I said, wrapping my arms around myself. "Why do you care?"

She opened her mouth to say something and then changed her mind. "You hate me."

Laura sat down on one of the chairs.

"I don't hate you, Colden. You know that."

"Do I?" I said, leaning down and petting Minnie. The pig was a nice distraction, I had to admit.

"Did you really think that I hated you?" I stared at her as if she'd grown an extra head.

"I can't imagine why," I said, holding up one finger, "You sneak all the good submissions away from me, you're always trying to push all my buttons, you're passive aggressive in emails, somehow you're always getting me to do the projects that you get assigned, and you always have this look on your face like you know something that I don't, or you think you're better than me. It's a lot, Laura. A lot." My chest heaved as I finished. I'd been holding that in for a long time. I didn't really have a whole lot of people to talk to about anything. Dad had been my sounding board for so long and I hadn't found anyone else in my life who could fill that void. I'd either talk to random people on the internet or to no one.

Laura stared at me for a second.

"Is that what you think I do?" She seemed horrified. What was even happening?

"It is, though. That's what you do. You don't like me and I don't like you." Why was she acting this way?

"Oh," she said, looking down at her hands in her lap. "Oh."

"I'm lost," I said.

"So am I," she said, her voice thick with emotion. "I didn't know that's what you thought of me." She was quiet for a long time. I didn't know what to say to her. I was completely puzzled.

"Don't you hate me?" I asked. I thought this was a known fact.

"No, Colden. I don't hate you. I mean, yes, I have done those things, but I didn't do them against you. I did them because I'm scared that I'm not going to make it. I have to prove myself. I have to prove that it wasn't a waste to go to school and try to make a go of it in publishing. That it wasn't a waste leaving my family and this." She gestured at the room, meaning the entire inn.

I had to sit down. There was too much to think about for me to concentrate on standing. I took the chair next to hers.

"You weren't fucking with me?"

"No. I was trying to get ahead. I guess you were sort of in the way. I mean, sure, I do feel competitive with you. I'm sure you do too. I'm not the only one who's snuck submissions and done sneaky things." She stared at me and I sputtered.

"Okay, fine. I've done it a few times. But not as many as you." I definitely didn't try to fuck her over as many times as she had to me. "And you're going to be fine. You're smart and you'll make it. You don't have to prove yourself to anyone." She shook her head.

"That's what you think. That family down there? They seem sweet and fun and goofy on the surface, but under that is a lot of expectation. A lot of history. You don't know what it's like to live and grow up knowing exactly what you're supposed to do and who you're supposed to be. And when you don't turn out to be that?" She sighed and looked out the window.

Minnie ran from me to Laura and back, as if she wanted to comfort both of us and couldn't decide who to focus on first.

"At least you have two living and involved parents," I snapped. "Count your fucking blessings, Laura. There are worse things out there than parental expectations." I got up from the chair and walked to the window. I couldn't look at her anymore.

"I didn't know anything about your parents. You never talk about yourself, Colden. You never share anything. I try to talk to you, all the time, and you give me *nothing*." One tear after another rolled down my cheeks. I angrily wiped them away.

"I didn't want you to know. I didn't want you to get to know me. You're just a coworker, Laura. Someone I don't even like. We just have to be able to share a workspace and that's it. We don't have to be friends." I felt her standing behind me and I turned slowly to meet her eyes.

"I wanted to get to know you, Colden. I tried. I know I'm not the easiest person to get along with. I take work way too seriously, I know that much. I need to lighten up. I know you probably don't want to be my friend, but I've wanted to be yours." I was shocked. It was as if she'd flipped my entire world upside down. I'd had it all wrong.

"Why do you want to be friends with me?" I couldn't imagine. I knew she already had friends. Probably rich friends that she could do rich people things with. Gold facials or whatever. I had no idea how rich people spent their money. I'd like to find out someday, though.

"Do you really want to do this?" Laura asked.

"I mean, you started it by barging into my room with the pig. You could have just left me alone." That was what I wanted. Right?

"Fine," she said, getting up. "I'll leave you alone, if that's what you want."

"Yup," I said, staring at the pattern in the carpet.

"Fine," she said again, and walked out the door, shutting it firmly behind her, leaving me and Minnie together.

"Alone at last," I said, petting Minnie, who sat down to my feet and put her chin in my lap.

"You can be my friend, Minnie. It would be fun to have a pig as a friend." She made a snuffling noise and smiled. I had decided: Pigs could smile.

"Can you fix my car?" I asked her. She didn't answer. "Okay, can you search for a secret hoard of gold? I'm sure there's some buried around her somewhere. You'd be like a truffle pig, only with money. I could train you and we'd travel all around the world having adventures finding gold. How does that sound?" Minnie closed her eyes and sighed, as if that idea contented her.

"It's a plan," I said.

~

SINCE I STILL DIDN'T HAVE MY car, I decided to take a walk to get away from the inn and the family that owned it for a while. I snuck out the back door and somehow managed not to see a single Sterling on my way. It wasn't as cold today, so the wind didn't freeze my nose instantly. The snow had melted a little in the sun, and the roads were clear, so I didn't have to worry about slipping on ice and slush. I had no idea where I was going, but I had my phone to navigate me back in case I got lost. It wasn't like there were a whole lot of places to go. The inn was down the street from the main area of town, if you could call it that. A gas station, a teeny-tiny bank, a grocery store, and a post office. That was pretty much it, at least I thought until I saw that there was a bitty coffee shop attached to the grocery store, along with a little shed that had a giant ice cream cone on top of it and a CLOSED sign across the door.

Coffee. Blessed coffee. I didn't drink it much, but I was hit with an overwhelming need for something rich and dark and full of caffeine. The smell alone made my mouth water. I pushed through the door, hearing the tinkle of a bell as I entered. The place was small, but so cozy. Only three tables, but there was a full-size espresso machine, and a full glass case of delectable-looking pastries. Sold. I was camping out here for the rest of the afternoon. I'd smartly shoved a book in one of my coat's giant pockets, so I was set.

I went to the counter to order and the young barista seemed excited to see me. Like, overly excited.

"How can I help you?" she chirped, her eyes bright behind clear-framed glasses. I'd put her age either late teens or early twenties. Still eager in her first job.

"Um, yeah, I'll have the gingerbread and white chocolate latte with a cherry Danish, please." I needed carbs and sugar and fat right now.

"Coming right up! What kind of milk did you want with that latte?" I looked at the selection and went with oat milk. I'd never tried it, but why not?

The Danish came on a plate and the latte came with an extra smile from the barista. She was the only one in the shop, but it wasn't like the line was twenty people deep. There were only three other people in here right now. Two teens who looked like they'd come here after school and an older man on a laptop. I sat at the only other available table and pulled out my book, settling in.

The bell above the door tinkled and I glanced up to see who it was. Michelle.

"Oh, hey, I didn't know you were over here. I just snuck over for a pick-me-up. I couldn't deal with my family anymore, and a bunch of people checked out and I had to clean and do check ins and I really need a coffee. Hi, Ashley." The last part was directed to the barista. "Can I get my usual?"

"Coming right up," Ashley said to Michelle.

"Do you mind if I join you while I wait? I'll be going back in a minute." I didn't mind. I liked Michelle. Even though she had a few too many stars in her eyes about the realities of living in a city as opposed to staying here.

"Yeah, go ahead." The older guy at the laptop coughed, as if he disapproved. Maybe he was writing a screenplay. There seemed to be a guy working on a screenplay in every café in all corners of the world.

"I heard about your car. That sucks." Yeah, it did. I was already tired of thinking about it.

"Yup," I said, sipping my latte. It was cool enough to drink now. I swallowed the caffeinated goodness and sunk my teeth into the Danish. Delicious. Completely perfect. I was going to order a second to take back with me for a midnight snack. Guess I was hanging out at The Sterling Inn again tonight. Unless I wanted to abandon my car, rent another, and bail. That prospect didn't seem so bad but, eventually, I was going to need my car.

"Is there anything I can do?" Michelle was such a peach.

We should definitely become friends. She was just the kind of person I should be friends with.

"Not unless you know where a pile of money that no one wants is buried. I'm going to train Minnie to be a money pig." Michelle blinked at me a few times and then she got it.

"Oh, right, like the pigs that look for truffles! That's not a bad idea. Put her to work." We both laughed at the idea of Minnie having a job.

"She should earn her keep, don't you think?" I said.

"Definitely."

Ashley, the barista, called out Michelle's order and she got up.

"I'll see you later? Uh, do you want me to tell anyone who asks if I've seen you that I haven't?" Yes, Michelle and I definitely should become friends.

"That would be amazing, thank you. I think your family is obsessed with me being a shiny new toy, and all the attention is a little much. I'd like a break." I'd also like to avoid questions about my car and sympathetic looks and pats on the shoulder and hugs. I just needed to be on my own. I was used to being alone, and I felt like I'd been surrounded by people forever, even though it had only been a few days.

"You got it. I'll also steer anyone away from the café if they ask about coming."

"Thank you," I said. "Seriously."

"You got it," she said, giving me a salute before she left. The old guy huffed again, annoyed by our talking voices. The teens were quiet, both heads pressed together over one of their phones, sharing a pair of earbuds. Cute.

I went back to my book and savored my latte. The combo of gingerbread and white chocolate was heavenly. I was going to have to start ordering this when I got back home. I fell into my book and got lost in the story. Movement made me look out the large front window that faced the street and little flakes of snow floated through the air and landed on the ground. The temperature had dropped enough that it was probably going to start sticking as the day wore on into night.

The moment was almost perfect. I had a Danish, I had coffee, I had a book, and I had a beautiful scene. This was very similar to what I'd imagined my Christmas vacation to be like. Ashley hummed softly as she cleaned the espresso machine and arranged the pastries and loaded the dishwasher.

The scene was sweet and peaceful, until someone walked through the door.

Laura.

I shoved my book in front of my face and wished there was somewhere for me to hide. The room was so small that there was no way she couldn't see me.

"Hey, Colden," she said, coming to stand in front of the table. "I have something for you."

I glared at her over the top of my book.

"What?" I said. I didn't want to see her. I had come her specifically to get away from her and the rest of her clan. Guess Michelle hadn't been able to keep her away.

"Merry Christmas, Grinch." She held up my car keys and jingled them before dropping them on the table where they clattered and made the older guy REALLY clear his throat in annoyance. I glared at the back of his head and then looked back at Laura in disbelief.

"What is this?"

"Your car is fixed. It's back in the parking lot at the inn."

I gaped at her.

"And who paid for it to get fixed?" Because that price Craig quoted me wasn't cheap. It was more than my rent for one month.

"Don't worry about it. It's been taken care of." Oh, shit. My initial feeling was nausea.

"You didn't," I said, needing her to tell me this was a joke. I didn't want them to do this for me. I didn't want them to do anything for me.

"I didn't, but Craig did, and I think you can probably thank my mom and maybe a few more of my relatives. I think it was a group effort. I thought you'd be happy. You were so upset about it earlier and now you don't have to worry about it." Was she serious? Now I was beholden to her family and I would have to find some way to pay them back. This was even worse than abandoning my car in a ditch somewhere, or pushing it into the ocean.

"I can't believe you let this happen." I snatched the keys from the table.

"You can't believe people would actually care about you and want to do nice things for you? What the hell, Colden?"

The older guy slammed his laptop shut, packed up his bag, and huffed away, as if we'd driven him to it. Whatever.

"Your family isn't my family. They don't know me. You don't know me. And now I'm beholden to them and I'll always be haunted by that debt. I'm going to pay them all back, but now I have to think about it. Jesus, Laura, can't you get that?" I closed my eyes and wanted to cry again. I could feel Ashley watching the exchange. She probably didn't get a lot of entertainment in here, so she was getting a good show today.

"You're being ridiculous. There are no strings with this. It's done. It's over. No one expects you to do anything. It's a present. Can't you accept that?"

"No," I said, slamming my book shut. "You just don't get it." I shoved my book back in my pocket and put the dishes on the counter for Ashley.

"Thank you," I said to her before I headed out the door, Laura following right behind me.

"Can't you just leave me be? I came all the way up here to get away from you, to get away from everything, and I got fucked over!" I yelled right outside the café. I'd had it.

Several passersby glared or stared at me. I didn't care if I looked like a jerk screaming in the streets. I was pissed and annoyed and no one was listening to me.

"Why can't you all just leave me alone?" I kept walking and I didn't know where to go because I didn't live here, but I stomped down the road and I heard Laura following me.

"Did you not hear me?" I asked, whirling around.

"I don't want you to get lost. You don't know where you're going," she said. Okay, that may be true, but I wasn't going to admit it.

"I don't care," I said, turning around and starting to walk again. I kept going, fueled by the caffeine buzz from the latte. Laura stayed behind me. I stomped and walked and got snow in my hair and on my eyelashes and there might have been a few tears in there too. I walked and Laura followed until I was on a side road that was barely plowed. I trudged and Laura trudged behind me until the road ended in what looked like an abandoned cabin.

"Are you ready to go back yet?" Laura asked, and I finally turned around. I really wanted to sit down, but there wasn't a place to do that, so I just leaned on one hip.

"I can't seem to make any of you understand how weird it's been for me to come up here and have all of you take care of me out of the blue. I'm just . . . it's weird, Laura. It's really weird for me. I think it would be weird for anyone to have a bunch of strangers treat her like one of their own. I'm not close to people. The only people I was ever truly close to left me or died." I crossed my arms and tried not to cry again. I was so tired of crying. I'd done more crying in the past few days than in the past few months. Like, what the fuck was this place doing to me?

"I understand that it's weird for you, but everyone really likes you and it's probably a little weird, but it's not unheard of. People give to strangers all the time. And you're not a stranger.

You're Colden, and they've gotten to know you and they want to help you and this will make your life easier. Also, it's the season of giving." Our eyes met and I knew what else she wasn't going to put words to: that her family had money and fixing my car was a drop in the bucket for them. I knew she was rich. She knew I knew she was rich, but it was just too uncomfortable to say out loud.

That was another reason I was so uncomfortable. The money. It mattered to me and it didn't matter to them, which made me feel gross inside.

"Come back to the inn with me. It's cold out here and I have to pee," she said.

"There's a tree right over there." There were a lot of trees.

"Yeah, I need a bathroom. I went on a class camping trip once and I found out that there was just an outhouse and I called my mom to come get me. I had to lie and say I was puking my guts out to get her to come, but she did. Then I got in big trouble for lying and being a baby." I couldn't lie, that was a cute story, but it didn't make me feel any better.

"Do you want to go back to the café? Have another cup of coffee? I'm really trying here, Colden. Can you give me something?" I clenched my teeth, but she did have a point. A tiny part of me knew that a lot of this was my issue and not hers, but I was stubborn as fuck and would rather die than admit I was wrong.

"Fine. But you're buying me another Danish." I definitely needed another Danish.

Chapter Five

WE MADE it back to the café without incident and Ashley was even more thrilled to see us. Probably hoping for more drama. I decided on a chai this time and Laura got us both Danishes.

The teens were gone, but there were a woman and someone who looked like he could be her son having coffee and laughing together. Sweet. There was a bitter taste on my tongue that I tried to wash away with a sip of the chai. It was creamy and full of spice. Ashley was a damn good barista. I hadn't had drinks this good in a long time.

"Okay. I let you buy me a Danish. Are you happy now?" I asked. Laura picked up her latte. She'd gotten three shots in it.

"Maybe," she said. "I'd be happier if you were okay."

I stared at her.

"Why do you care about me?"

"Are we back to this again? You have a really warped idea of yourself, Colden." I wanted to yell at her again, but I kept my mouth shut. I didn't want to abandon my Danish. I shoved half of it in my mouth so I wouldn't make a snappy retort.

"I would like to be your friend, Colden. I really would. You're funny and smart and really fucking good at your job.

You see the magic in a submission that I might pass by because I can't see past a few errors. You don't give yourself enough credit."

"Don't act like you know me," I said, through a mouthful of Danish. I didn't like other people telling me about myself. Let me tell you about myself.

"I'd like to get to know you. If you'd let me." I wiped my mouth and sipped my drink, thinking about it. She did push all my freaking buttons, that was for sure. And I was never going to get over what she'd done to me at work. But we had had a good time last night with the frosting fight, and I was starting to see that the face she put on at work might not be her true self. Laura bundled up her personality in layers and I had to admit, I was intrigued to find out what was beneath the façade I saw every day. Plus, I guess I owed her for helping out with my car.

"Fine. We can attempt to be friends."

"Don't look so excited about it, Colden." I liked the way she said my name, which only grated on me more.

"I'm so excited to be your friend," I said sarcastically, and then flashed her a smile and two thumbs up.

"I'm beginning to regret my decision," she said.

∼

I WAS out of practice making friends, apparently. After the coffee was gone and I didn't have anything to do with my hands, I didn't know what to do. We sat there and kind of stared at each other.

"Sooo," she said, drawing out the word.

"So," I said. "Uh, what are your opinions on potatoes?"

She stared at me as if I'd spoken another language.

"Potatoes?"

"Yeah. You can do so much with them. Fries, chips, baked potatoes, gnocchi. It's a versatile thing, the potato."

She blinked a few times and then smiled slowly.

"Well, I prefer garlic mashed potatoes over potatoes with no garlic. Garlic makes everything better." I hated that I agreed with her. "Ketchup or no ketchup on fries?"

"I'm pro-ketchup."

"I'm anti-ketchup. Let the potatoes stand on their own merit," she said.

I narrowed my eyes. "I'm not sure if I can be friends with someone who doesn't like ketchup."

"I eat it on hot dogs. Just not on potatoes. That's just wrong." I growled and she laughed. "I didn't know you had such intense ketchup opinions."

"I have many opinions," I said. "You sure you're ready to hear them all?"

She grinned. "Bring it."

We spent the next however long arguing about condiments. I'd literally never talked with another person about mayonnaise this intensely before. In the background, Ashley leaned on the counter while pretending to clean and listening to the whole thing. People came and went from the café, especially as it started to get dark, but Laura and I kept talking and arguing about which was the best brand of hot sauce.

A sound made me jump and she looked down at her phone.

"Oh, shit. Uh, I was supposed to be helping serve dinner apparently. I have to get back to the inn. You want to come with me, friend?" I made a face and put the dishes on the counter for Ashley.

"Thanks," I said, as she grabbed them from me.

"Come back anytime," she said in an overly perky voice.

"I will," I said. There was an upside to having the Sterlings fix my car: now I could physically leave.

Laura and I shuffled through the slush to get back to the inn.

"Are you going to stay?" she asked me, and I didn't have an answer for her.

"I don't know. I feel like I have to now, to thank your family, but it will make me feel even more like a leech, eating your food and sleeping in your bed for free." We reached the inn and stood there for a moment, looking at it all lit up.

"It's really beautiful here," I said, looking at her in the glow of the lights strung along the porch.

"I think I'm so used to it that I don't see it anymore. It's cool to see it through someone else's eyes." I could feel her watching me and I met her eyes.

"You're lucky. To have them. To have this." I gestured to the inn. I had nothing from my family. My dad's house, the home I'd grown up in, had been taken by the bank when I couldn't come up with money for the mortgage. I hadn't been able to do anything to stop it.

"I guess," she said, and I wanted to smack her. She had no idea what she had, which pissed me off. She had everything and she couldn't fucking see it.

"I'm going to check on my car," I said. I wasn't ready to be faced with what I didn't have in my own life yet.

"Okay," Laura said, getting the hint. "I'll let you know what the specials are when you come to dinner." I didn't want to come to dinner. I wanted to get in my car and drive and forget about this place.

I headed for my car and got in, turning it on. It purred to life like it was brand new. It even smelled new, as if it had been detailed. I looked around and even in the dark, I could tell it had been. Fucking hell. What was wrong with these people?

It was so damn tempting to back out of the driveway and head to Boston, but all my shit was in the room. I couldn't leave my books, even though they'd probably mail them to me. Assholes.

Sighing and resting my head on the steering wheel, I closed my eyes and tried to figure out what my options were. Basically, unless I wanted to abandon my shit in the room, I had to get out of the car and go back to the inn and face all the people who had done something so kind for me.

Let's get this over with.

∾

"YOU'RE BACK!" Michelle said, rushing over to me.

"I am?" I said. She had her hands out like she wanted to inspect me for injuries or something.

"Are you okay?" She seemed overly concerned.

"I'm fine?" I said, taking my jacket off and folding it over my arm.

"Oh, good. We were worried."

"You were?" Had I missed something? I'd only been out in my car for a few minutes. Laura must have come in and told them where I was.

"I mean, I was." Her cheeks turned red and I was beginning to suspect something when Minnie came barreling out of the dining room to crash into my legs and nearly knock me over.

"Oh my god, hi, yes, I missed you too," I said, reaching down and scratching her with both hands. It was strange how used to a giant pig you could get in a short period of time.

"I think someone missed you," Laura's voice said. I looked up to find her dressed in the server uniform.

"Hey," I said, even though I'd seen her just a few minutes ago.

"You coming to dinner?" she asked. Michelle coughed next to me.

"Yeah, just going to go upstairs and switch my boots out." I blew Minnie a kiss and she ran back into the dining room.

"Your bed is all made," Michelle called out, as I ascended the stairs.

"Oh, thanks." I wondered if she'd made it up for me. "You didn't have to. I can make it up myself."

"It was no problem." She seemed a little breathless and my suspicions increased.

"Thanks," I said again, giving her a little wave as I kept walking up the stairs. Michelle having a crush on me was a complication I hadn't seen coming. I wasn't reading too much in that, wasn't I? Sure, I'd been oblivious in the past, but that was pretty clear-cut. Yikes.

The suite I'd come to think of as mine had clearly been cleaned and when I went to the bedroom I found the bed made, a towel swan, and a plate of cookies on the pillow. That was as clear a sign as any. Sure, Michelle was cute, and fun, but I wasn't into her that way and I didn't think that was going to change. Plus, even if I was, how could it work? She lived and worked here and there was no way I could handle a long-distance thing. Hell no.

I blew out a noisy breath and switched my shoes and hung up my coat. If I wasn't so hungry, I'd hang out up here longer, but I was hungry, so downstairs I went.

Nearly every head snapped in my direction and I had to look down to make sure it wasn't that dream where you walk into a room and you're naked and everyone else is clothed. Nope, I had jeans and a shirt on. Phew.

"Colden, it's wonderful to see you," Laina said, coming over and putting her hand on my shoulder. Ugh, I didn't want to talk to her. The car thing was going to come up inevitably.

"Would you like to talk for a moment? Laura filled me in on how you felt about the car."

"Sure," I said, and we went back into the kitchen where

Laura's dad Antonio was singing and sautéing. She took me all the way to the back, near the laundry room and next to the walk-in freezer.

"It's a little quieter out here," she said, but tossed a glare at the sound of her husband's singing.

"It's a good thing I love him," she said with a sigh, before returning to look at me.

"So, I understand that you were a little uneasy about the car situation and I just wanted to assure you that we don't expect you to pay us back. Craig did the work out of the goodness of his heart. It's what Sterlings do." Was she going to whip out the family crest?

"I understand that but it still . . . it feels like charity. And I'm already staying here for free, eating your food, taking up a room you could be making money on." My stomach kept knotting in new and unpleasant ways, and I wanted this moment to end. This was horrible.

"I know you had this grand plan of spending Christmas by yourself, but I'm glad you're here, Colden. I'm happy to have you. I think Laura is too." Wait a minute. We were changing directions here.

"That doesn't mean you should hand me free stuff and pay for my car to get fixed. I just . . . I don't like feeling like a burden." There was a lump in my throat that threatened to choke me.

"You're not a burden, Colden. You're a joy to have around. We're so happy to have you with us." I thought she was going to hug me again, but she didn't. She stood there and waited.

"I'm not ungrateful. I'm so grateful. Beyond words. I'm just not used to it." I had gotten out of practice with people caring for me. I just really missed my dad. Times like this reminded me of the wound in my chest where parts of my heart used to be that were gone now. There were days when they didn't hurt with every breath I took, but today was not one of those days.

"Laura hasn't told me, but do you have any family?" I knew this question was going to come up. It always did. Surprising that Laura didn't tell her mom.

"My mother was never around and I lost my dad to a brain tumor three years ago. So it's just me." Saying it was so sad, it was hard to believe that it was my actual life. If someone else told me that story, I'd feel sorry and want to hug them.

"I'm so sorry about both your parents. That's not easy for anyone to go through, at any age." I shrugged because what else was there to say about it? I'd gotten through it? I was still breathing? I had to keep moving because if I stood still too long and thought about it, I might not want to go on?

"I'm sorry if we made you uncomfortable with the car, we should have asked, but I saw a chance to do a good deed and took it." I got what she was saying, and I knew in some ways, I was being a pain about it, but I didn't know how else to be.

"It's okay. It was just a shock and I'm still processing."

Laina gave me a warm smile.

"Take all the time you need. And I really wish you would stay with us until Christmas. You don't have to decide right now, but I'm extending the invitation. We would all love to have you." I couldn't give her an answer to that right now. My initial feeling was to reject the offer and go back to Boston, but something stopped me from saying that right out. Maybe it was hunger. Maybe it was the warmth that I felt when I was around them. Maybe it was curiosity to see Laura interact in her natural habitat. Whatever it was, I was sticking around. For now.

"Come on, let's go have dinner," Laina said, leading me back through the kitchen and into the dining room. I was seated next to Laura's Uncle Dan, who I hadn't had a ton of interaction with yet, but who I was curious to get to know. Being trans myself and everything.

Laura came around and told us the specials, but nothing struck my fancy so I scanned the menu.

"What are you going to get?" Uncle Dan asked, leaning over a little.

"I have no idea. Everything here is so good."

"The baked chicken dinner is a religious experience, let me tell you. Add the black truffle garlic mashed potatoes. You'll think you died and went to heaven." That did sound amazing.

I cleared my throat after I put in my order.

"So, um, I'm not sure if Laura has told you?"

"That you're nonbinary? Yes, she has. Are you also trans?" I nodded. It had taken me a while to come to terms with using the word "transgender" to describe myself, but I'd gotten here.

He grinned at me and a dimple popped in each cheek.

"It's nice to have someone else who understands, isn't it?" Yeah, it was. I breathed out and some of the knots in my chest started to loosen.

"I didn't come out until I was in my twenties. It was different then, but I'll never forget that my parents were on board immediately. They knew nothing, but they were getting books and joining groups and it was a little much, actually." He laughed.

"Wow, that's great. My dad was supportive too. At first he asked me if I needed any money for surgery, because he had some set aside for an emergency." I loved that memory. "Not going to lie, I'm pretty sure that he was a little relieved when I told him I didn't think I was going to need surgery right then, but that it was good to know if I did someday, that it was there." I wished I still had that money, but it was long gone, along with the house I'd tried to keep, but had also lost. I needed to get off this morbid memory lane.

"We trans people have to stick together. Let me know if anyone says anything, or makes you feel weird and I'll go to bat for you." I thanked him for that. He switched topics and started talking about his girlfriend, who was in Philly with her family, but who he couldn't wait to see. They'd met online in a Dungeons and Dragons forum and had fallen in love. I had to admit, my cold, dead heart warmed up and grew a few sizes as he told me about her.

"You going to help with the wreaths tonight?" he asked as dessert was served a while later.

"Oh, uh, I don't know." I'd forgotten about the group activities. At least it wasn't Christmas Charades?

"You don't have to be artistic. We'll teach you how to do them." I wasn't sure about that, but I didn't really see a choice, since they'd all pitched in to fix my car. I owed them at least this.

"Sure, why not?" I said.

"What are you doing?" Laura said, coming to deliver my dessert of coconut mango pie that they called "pina colada pie" and sounded like the most delicious thing I'd ever heard of.

"Helping with wreaths," I said.

"Oh, good." She walked away and I stared after her.

"You okay?" Dan asked, and I ripped my attention from Laura and back to the delicious dessert.

"Yeah, fine," I said, stabbing my fork into the pie and scooping up a huge piece.

˜

LAURA PLAYED jaunty tunes on the piano while we wrapped cold, damp pine branches into wire frames and then added sprigs of real berries and bows. It was harder than it looked, and my fingers were sticky with sap, and I'd almost touched my eyes at least three times and had to pull my hand away at the last minute.

I had to admit, I was having a good time. Everyone took

pity on me as a novice wreath-maker and was giving me so much praise that it bordered on ridiculous.

"Great job, that looks amazing," Michelle said as she went to get more supplies from the big table covered in branches and bows and berries.

"Thanks," I said, not meeting her eyes. I didn't want to give her a false impression of my feelings, but I also didn't want to be a bitch, either. It was a fine line to walk and I didn't know if I was doing a good job.

I propped up my finished wreath and had to admit that it wasn't that bad. I didn't think anyone would be upset with it. I carried it to the pile of finished wreaths and added it. I'd already done three and I was ready to be done, so I hit the bathroom to try and remove as much of the sap as possible before I drifted over to the piano.

"You should have a tip jar," I said, as she paused between songs and drank from a bottle of water.

"No one would tip me. They're all family, except for you and like five other people." Customers at the inn were scarce and were usually coming or going on journeys to other places. Almost the entire inn was Sterlings, Minnie, and me. I was completely outnumbered.

"I'd tip you," I said, and wanted to take it back the second the words were out of my mouth. It almost sounded like I was flirting, which I definitely didn't want to do. Not with Michelle, sure as hell not with Laura.

"Your uncle Dan is cool. We talked a lot about trans stuff."

She plinked out a little tune and then another, not playing anything in particular. "Yeah, he is. He was the first trans person I ever really met, and I think it's because of him that I realized I was a lesbian. He opened the door for a lot of us in the family." She looked up at me and I froze for a moment, leaning on the piano. Those eyes of hers were just . . . had I ever noticed them this way before? I'd seen her nearly every day and I had never really paid attention to them. Yes, they were brown, but more than that. They had the smallest flecks of bright gold in them and the subtlest dark brown ring around the iris. Not just brown at all.

Someone yelled something in our direction and Laura snapped her eyes shut and turned toward the heckler. It was Mel, one of her aunts, and her wife Sue, yelling out requests.

"Back to work," she said with a sigh, as she started to play "Baby It's Cold" and there was a chorus of boos.

"What's up with that?" I asked as Laura played.

"They do this every year. Let the discourse begin. The yelling will start to escalate any minute now." She shut her eyes and gave her body over to the music and I watched as the discussion did escalate. Wow, this family could really have a disagreement in dramatic fashion.

"You have to take the song in the historical context it was written!" someone yelled.

"It's still a shitty song!" someone yelled back.

"Language!" Lillian called out. I'd never seen anything like it. I'd thought things would come to blows, but then Laina brought out eggnog, and everyone agreed to disagree for another year and toasted one another.

"You family is bizarre," I said, as Laura took another break and looked over her shoulder at them.

"Yeah, they are." Laina came over with two mugs of eggnog. I didn't need to ask if there was rum in it. I could smell it a mile away.

"Be careful. Your father was generous with the booze this year."

"You say that every year," Laura said, sniffing the mug and wincing before taking a sip and sighing in pleasure. I didn't want to admit that I'd never had eggnog before. I didn't like the idea of a drink with eggs in it, and the word "nog" was weird. I looked into the cup with the thick cream-colored liquid that was studded with sprinkles of cinnamon and nutmeg. The smell alone was enough to make me try it and when I sipped, I was surprised. I'd thought I would taste egg, but it wasn't like that. The little hit of spiced rum warmed my throat and belly.

"Oh, that is really good." I'd have to be careful, because it had more than a little bit of rum in every cup.

"Be careful," Laura warned, before she took a dainty sip of her cup. "You don't know how many relatives have gotten wasted on this stuff over the years. Last year Mel and Sue ended up singing karaoke so loud that the neighbors complained. It was a whole big thing." I kind of wished I could go back in time and see that. Mel and Sue were my two new favorite people and I wished aunt adoption was a thing, because I wanted to have them as aunts.

Laura had no idea what she had, and if I sat down and thought about it, I'd get really angry, so I had to not think about it. She was so lucky and so fortunate to have such a big family around her who completely adored and supported anything she wanted to do. It wasn't her fault, but I could feel jealousy simmering deep in my stomach along with the eggnog.

"Is it bad that I want to get them drunk so they'll do it again?" I said, and Laura laughed.

"Just be careful what you wish for."

∼

WARM AND SLEEPY from the eggnog buzz, I went back upstairs a few hours later. All I wanted to do was sit and read, and just as I'd settled in after a shower, there was a knock at the door. I went to look out the peephole, but there was no one there. Curious, I opened the door and found a tray outside my room with a little note.

I picked up the tray and brought it inside. Under the lid

was a plate of cookies, some of which I had decorated. There was also a glass of ice-cold milk.

Thought you might need a little something to soak up all the rum in the eggnog.

-Laura

Weird. Why wouldn't she just have given me the tray herself instead of dingdong ditching it? Puzzled, I brought the tray to the little table next to the chair I liked to read in.

I had been craving a little something and this was perfect. As if she'd read my mind and knew what I needed. I set the note aside after admiring her perfect handwriting for a moment. Of course she had impeccable penmanship. Was there anything she couldn't excel at?

The cookies made the perfect companion to the lesbian historical romance that I'd been slow reading because it was so good. This was pretty near what I had wanted for my Christmas. I'd kind of lucked into getting it in an indirect way. Sure, I had to talk to a bunch of people and now I had to try to be friends with Laura and I was in debt to a bunch of people for fixing my car, but otherwise, I'd gotten my Christmas wish, as sappy as that sounded.

I shoved another cookie into my mouth and went back to my book.

Chapter Six

"You want to do something later?" Laura asked after breakfast the next morning. I'd thanked her for the cookies and milk and she waved me off, saying it was nothing. Speaking of the eggnog, I'd woken up with a headache and a rolling stomach, but a nice breakfast and some extra-strength painkillers had done the trick.

My plan had been to read at the café for a little while, take a walk, and then come back to read some more and maybe a long bubble bath with more books. I also should probably drive my car a little bit and see some more of the town.

"What the hell is there to do around here?" They didn't even have a movie theater or a bowling alley. Nearly everything else was only open in the summer.

"Well, I need to go to the post office, the bank, I need some groceries from town, and wiper fluid for my car. If I buy you lunch, will you come?"

"How about I buy you lunch for a change?" I said. I had enough cash for that.

"Deal," she said. "Meet me in the lobby in an hour?" I agreed and went back upstairs to my room.

What the hell had I just agreed to? Less than a week ago, if Laura would have asked me to have lunch with her I would have told her to kiss my ass. Well, I wouldn't have put it like that, but I definitely would have turned her down. This place was affecting my brain.

The familiar feeling in my stomach had returned, so I mentally tested out my pronouns and 'they' was working more for me today. I tried to convince my brain that 'she' could work, but there was that gross sick feeling that meant it was wrong for now. That could change in a few hours, and it had before. Sometimes I hated it. At least I knew that Laura would respect the change in pronouns, and Dan would go to bat for me if anyone else had a problem with it. I missed my pin, because it made the announcement for me.

I read until I needed to meet Laura, and I was excited to see more of the state. I'd kind of been on autopilot when I'd driven up here, and I'd been so focused on getting to the cottage that I hadn't really been looking at my surroundings.

"Hey, you okay?" Laura said.

"Yeah, why?" I asked. It was like she'd sensed my gender feels.

"You just look like you're upset about something."

"No, I mean, not really. Just missing my pronoun pin. I was hoping that I'd be good with 'she' for the whole time I was here, but I guess not? So, 'they', if you don't mind." I hated asking. I still wasn't used to it, and I put up with a lot of misgendering just because it was easier than fighting with people.

"Got it. I'll let everyone know. We've got a family group text." She got right on her phone and spent a moment sending the message. "All set. I'll remind anyone who forgets."

And that was that. We put our coats and boots on and headed out to Laura's car. It was better in the snow than mine.

"I'm still mad," I said. "About the fixing my car thing."

"Well, do you want me to smash the shit out of it?" Laura asked, as she backed out of the parking lot and pulled onto the main road. The weather had warmed up a tiny bit, and the roads were clear. Snow was expected again tomorrow. If this kept up, it was going to be a white Christmas.

"No, I don't want you to smash my car. I just wish it was fixed in a different way, that's all." I wish I was the one who had orchestrated and paid for it, but what was done was done, and I guess I couldn't go back, so it was ridiculous to keep obsessing over it. No one else was making a big deal out of it.

Laura didn't respond as she headed down the road to the post office first.

"Do you want to stay in the car?" she asked.

"No, I'm not a dog. I'll come in." Sure, I'd brought a book, but I also did want to see more of the town and the sun was out, so this seemed as good a time as any.

The post office was actually attached to someone's house, which was really weird. The place was absolutely tiny with only a very few boxes. It was crowded with people mailing Christmas packages and cards at the last minute. Great.

"So, most of these are international," the woman ahead of us said, as she plunked down a stack of cards. I almost screamed. She started filling out customs forms and I looked at Laura.

"That's Susan Miller. Her daughter and I were in the same grade. She was really conservative and wouldn't let a boy anywhere near her house, but what she didn't know was that her daughter and I were fooling around during every sleep-over." I almost choked when I tried to inhale a breath as Susan chattered away to the postal worker about her family and her Christmas plans.

"Good for you," I said to Laura. "What happened to the daughter?"

"She went to Smith and only visits every few years with her

wife and kids." Nice. "Susan still tells everyone they're just best friends who live together."

I snorted. Finally, Susan Miller finished what she was doing and said a polite hello to Laura, and went on her merry way, so I didn't have to be introduced or make small talk.

Laura got stamps and mailed some things and then we were off to the bank to do the deposit. The bank wasn't attached to someone's house, but it was just about the size of someone's living room and there were only two tellers.

Laura chatted with the teller, who had known her since she was *this big* and wouldn't stop telling stories about Laura when she was little, which Laura hated and I definitely enjoyed.

"Did you really have green hair? And an eyebrow ring?" I couldn't imagine it. I tried to picture it and couldn't. Although, if anyone could rock green hair, it would be Laura.

"Yes." I stared really close above her left eyebrow and saw the tiniest little dot that might have been where a piece of metal once lived. Cool.

"What kind of green? Like, dark green, or light green?"

Laura glared at me.

"It was lime green, okay? Lime green. I had to bleach the shit out of it before I could get the color on and I think my scalp is still fried." I tried to imagine a teenage Laura wandering around town with lime green hair and a surly expression on her face and couldn't.

"Well, I'm learning all kinds of things about you, Laura Sterling. Are we going to see your high school math teacher at the grocery store?"

Laura rolled her eyes and pulled onto the road again, looking both ways.

"Probably."

~

WE DID END up seeing her high school math teacher. And her English teacher. And her French teacher. Going through the grocery store with her was an experience. It took five times longer because she had to stop and chat with nearly everyone who passed us with a cart. I got introduced a few times, but people seemed more interested in Laura than me, which was fine.

She asked about their kids and jobs and plans for Christmas and listened and was soft and sweet and it was a whole other side of Laura I'd never seen. Yet another layer. At work she was quick and decisive and mostly kept her head down.

"Oh my god, no more," she said, when we reached the other side of the store. "Seriously, if I see one more person from high school, I'm going to lose my mind. A lot of these people were assholes to me and now they pretend we were buddies and it's like no, Courtney, you treated me like shit for four years." I laughed under my breath as she threw several cans of cranberry sauce in the cart.

"Doesn't your dad make fresh sauce?" I asked. I'd already had it the other night.

"Yeah, but people love the canned stuff, so here we are. We're also doing mac and cheese next week and he wanted to make sure we had some options for anyone who's vegan, so I have to find vegan cheese here somewhere." I highly doubted the store had vegan cheese, but I was proved wrong when we found it in the natural section.

"Well, would you look at that," she said, grabbing several packages and sticking them in the cart. "Do you need anything?"

"Nope." My (perishable) groceries were in the walk-in freezer at the inn, and anything that could keep was in my trunk. I'd snuck a few of the snacks up to my room and put a few drinks in the fridge. At least those wouldn't go to waste.

Laura sighed as we made our way to the checkout area and then took everything out to her car.

"Okay, that's done. How about we drop this off at the inn and then we can do whatever we want. I can show you the wonders of rural Maine." Her voice dripped with sarcasm.

"As long as there are no bears. Are there bears here?"

Laura laughed. "I mean, sure, people go bear hunting, but I've never seen one. It's not a problem we really deal with. Deer and moose on the other hand? Yes."

We'd only had deer where I grew up. You had to be so careful driving on certain roads at night.

"What about reindeer?" I asked.

"Haha, very funny, this isn't the North Pole, Colden."

"Well, Maine is basically Canada, so what do I know?"

She rolled her eyes and groaned as we drove back to the inn.

Laura and I dragged everything through the back and made our escape again before anyone noticed.

"Seriously, I have no idea how we pulled that off," she said in a hushed voice, as if angry relatives or her parents could hear her.

"Did you grow up here?" I knew from talking to Laina that the family lived in the gorgeous house next door to the inn, and several other relatives lived in houses down the street, or nearby.

"Yup. They all assumed I would come back after college. Even asked me if I'd do the marketing and handle the website and so forth, but I said that wasn't what I wanted. Let's just say it didn't go over well." It was difficult to reconcile that story with all the people I'd met. They didn't seem pushy at all, but maybe the pressure had been more passive aggressive. More subtle.

"Don't you have enough relatives to run the place?" It seemed like there were plenty of Sterlings around already.

"Yeah, but it's supposed to be me. I'm an only child and they'd wanted it for me ever since I was little. I'd grown up running up and down those stairs and playing hide-and-seek in the empty rooms. The inn was like my playground, but I grew up. I knew it wasn't what I wanted. Firstly, it's a fuck ton of responsibility, and I just don't have the passion for it. I didn't think I should do something that my heart wasn't in. My parents told me that I'd learn to love it. I disagreed." My dad had always told me that I could do whatever I wanted and he'd support me. I asked him if he meant *anything* and he said anything legal, but other than that, if I was doing what I truly wanted to, that didn't hurt me or anyone else? He was in.

"How long did it take them to get over it?"

Laura gave me a look. "They didn't get over it. They're just sneakier about their guilt trips now." I hadn't seen any, but maybe because I'd been so self-absorbed in the past few days. I made a note to pay attention more to Laina and Laura's interactions.

"It's my legacy," she said. "But I don't want it."

"With great power comes great responsibility," I said.

"Is that a JFK quote?"

"No, it's from Spiderman."

Laura snorted and kept driving.

"So, there are only like six places for lunch, so I will let you decide. There is pizza, a pub, a café with sandwiches and stuff, a disgusting chain restaurant, and a Thai place." I settled on the pub, since I was feeling like I wanted something warm and comforting.

Laura parked the car and we got a table at the pub. It was a tiny place, but they played good music and had a great mixed-drinks menu.

"The French onion soup here is to die for," Laura said. "It's what I always get when I'm here." That sounded perfect, so we both ordered that and salads and got drinks.

"Were you out in high school?" I asked. I knew so little about her.

"No, it wasn't until college. You?"

"Yeah, but only to a few friends, and my dad. Once I got to college I went a little wild." Oh, those had been the days.

"Oh, really? I would have liked to see that." She sipped her drink smirked at me.

"Let's just say if there was a girl on campus who liked girls or girl-adjacent people, I probably made out with her." And did other stuff. So what, I'd been a slut for a while. No regrets. Well, except for a few times, but I learned from all those experiences.

"Wow. I'm a little jealous."

Was she jealous of me or the girls I made out with? I didn't want to know the answer to that question.

"I was a little more subdued in college. I didn't want anything to distract me from my goals. Boring, I know, but I was a lot more uptight back then."

"You used to be *more* uptight?"

"Shut up, yes. I wasn't much fun to be around." I sipped at my drink so I wouldn't say something mean. "I can hear you making comments in your head. You might not be saying them out loud, but they're all over your face."

"I'm sorry that I can't control what my face does. I've tried and it doesn't work." I'd always been like that. I was one of the worst liars in the entire world, mostly because I couldn't hide my emotions.

"Fine, let's talk about something else. When did you figure out your gender?"

"That came later. I thought I was a cis lesbian for a long time, but then I became friends with a lot of trans and nonbinary people, yes, I kissed a lot of them too, and I started thinking and questioning and it sort of came at me slowly. I stuck with the same pronouns I'd had for a long time, but then someone used 'they' for me and I heard it and I realized that I liked it. So then I experimented with using that exclusively, but there were still times when I ached to be called 'she' so then I just kind of switched back and forth. It sounds confusing, but believe me, it was worse for me than it was for anyone else. My dad used to ask me every day what I was using and he'd write it down to make sure he didn't slip up. Even though it wouldn't have mattered if he did. I knew he was doing his best and he loved me." Talking about Dad wasn't easy. I usually cried when I did, which was why I didn't, most of the time.

"What happened to him? If it's not too hard to talk about."

"Brain tumor." That was pretty much the end of the conversation with most people.

"I'm so sorry. That's horrible."

The soup arrived and saved me from having to go on about my horrible life. Laura and I were consumed with trying to eat the soup that was thick with bread and gooey cheese. Not the easiest to eat, but it was so freaking good. Exactly what I'd needed.

"Do you want to talk about your dad, or do you want to talk about something else?" Laura asked, as she ate her salad.

"Something else, please." I was glad she'd asked instead of barging ahead.

"Okay, are you going to play Christmas Charades tonight? I mean, you don't really have an option, but if you really want to get out of it, I can tell them you have a migraine." I stared at her. I'd forgotten about the activities.

"Is it possible to watch without participating?" Because it honestly sounded amazing. With her family, it was bound to be hilarious as well.

"Nope. You don't get to just watch. The only one who's exempt is Gen, because it can get pretty loud and raucous. She likes to watch, though, and sometimes guesses, as long as she has her headphones on."

"Damn." I guess I wasn't getting out of it unless I was willing to lie about having a migraine or something else. "I'll think about it."

"Fair enough. You know it won't be too high-pressure. Just silly fun with the Sterlings. *Some* people take it too far, but you can just ignore them."

"Do you get competitive?" I asked. I bet she did. She was ruthless when it came to work, so why would this be different?

"Let's just say my team always wins. One way or another."

"Story checks out," I said, as we both finished our soup and salads.

"Do you want to get something sweet?" I said, and I flinched at the way it came out. Almost sexual. Ew, I didn't want to do anything sexual with Laura.

"I could definitely go for something," she said, grabbing the dessert menu. "What about pie? Cake?"

"I doubt it will be as good as your dad's, but I could go for some cake." I'd had far too many cookies in the past few days. I had been neglecting cake as my favorite dessert.

"Want to try the apple spice cake with cream cheese frosting?" That sounded perfect, so we ordered a slice each.

"You didn't want to share?" Laura asked.

"No, I never want to share cake. Other things, yes, but never cake. I get my own piece."

She leaned one elbow on the table and sat forward.

"What kind of things would you share?"

"Mostly everything but cake. I mean, I know I'm an only child, but I do know how to share."

She laughed a little.

"Why do they always say that about only children? Like we never interacted with anyone. I mean, I had my cousins all around all the time. I might not have any siblings, but I was around plenty of other kids and was taught to share." I didn't like the way I felt when she talked about her big family. When

I'd been growing up it hadn't been that much of a big deal that I wasn't from a big family, but as I'd gotten older, the difference between my family and someone else's got starker. It was even worse now. I felt like most of the time I had nothing to talk about. I didn't have nieces or nephews or cousins or sisters or brothers or parents or grandparents. None of it. I wasn't going to be spending any holidays with anyone. I spent my holidays alone and trying not to cry. This was the first year that I'd felt kind of okay about being alone and here I was, still alone, and just more aware of it.

"Are you okay?" Laura reached out and touched my arm. I didn't pull away.

"I mean, no. Honestly. I just have my moments when I get sad. I was just having a moment. It will pass." Our cake arrived, which broke up the moment a little.

"I'm sorry. I can talk about my family less if it bothers you." I stabbed my fork into the cake.

"No, it's fine. I can't avoid everyone who has a family. It's fine." The cake was delicious, but I wasn't enjoying it.

"I'm sorry," she said again, and I wished she'd stop apologizing.

"Are you going to be glad to get back to work?" she asked, after a few moments of tense silence.

"Yeah, I think so." I did miss work, even if it stressed me out. It gave me something to do during the day, and by the time I got home I was usually so exhausted that I didn't have time to think about my sad and miserable existence. Maybe I should get a dog or something. Or perhaps a pig.

"I'm looking forward to the rush of new year's submissions. That should be good."

I cringed. "You know what that means? Lots of garbage. Should we do Worst Of again?" In an effort to maintain sanity when filtering through submissions, we picked the best of the worst that came through the inbox and made up little certificates each quarter and had a little ceremony with donuts and coffee and we all dressed up in gowns and suits and finery as if it was an awards show and we all gave little acceptance speeches. It was totally dorky and fun, but I loved it.

"Absolutely, the year wouldn't be the same without it." That got us on a less fraught conversation topic and we reminisced about the most awful submissions we'd ever gotten. That included several that had come in the mail with strange gifts, including a hand-drawn portrait of our boss that looked like it was drawn by a disturbed child, but the author was a middle-aged man.

We finished our lunch and I wasn't ready to go back to the inn, and I didn't think she was either.

"Want to see my high school?" she asked, as we got in the car.

"Yeah, I do," I said, and it was the truth. I did. I wanted to know what Laura was like when she'd been an awkward teenager in this small town where she was related to so many people.

Laura drove and finally arrived at her alma mater, Seaside High School. Of course it was called that.

"What's your mascot?" I asked, as we sat in the car in the empty parking lot.

Laura pointed to the sign. "Tigers."

"Oh, that's boring. I would have thought it was the lobsters or moose or mosquitoes or something."

Laura laughed.

"I'm just picturing the guy who wore the tiger costume dressing up as a mosquito." She laughed so hard that tears ran down her face and it made me laugh, seeing her like that.

"You said you were uptight in high school?" I said, after we'd both calmed down.

"Yeah, little bit. Would you believe I was the vice president of the student council, won the spelling bee, and also was the secretary of the National Honor Society?"

"This is shocking information," I said in a deadpan voice.

"I know, I know. I'm predictable. What were you like in high school?"

High school felt like it was a million years ago, even though it wasn't that long.

"I don't know, I wasn't anything special. I had friends and I hung out and read a bunch of books, but I wasn't in any clubs or anything. I kind of drifted around." I was boring.

"I bet a lot of people had crushes on you."

I looked at her as if she'd lost her mind. Was that a joke?

"Yeah, I don't think so. Or if they did, no one told me. I tried to date guys, but I had two dates and one bad kiss and that was it for me. I decided that I wasn't going to be with anyone and then I kissed a girl and the world opened up." I'd been sixteen and it was kind of a joke between me and one of my friends. It was a sleepover and she'd been drinking (I hadn't) and she dared me to kiss her and I realized that fuck yes, I really wanted to kiss her. So I did.

The next day, I mentioned the kiss and either she didn't remember, or she pretended not to. We drifted apart when she joined the track team and abandoned me for people who enjoyed running. Part of me wanted to go on social media and see what she was doing right now.

Laura and I talked more about high school and she told me about her clubs and how she was an overachiever because she was an only child and always wanted her parent's approval. I'd never felt that pressure from my dad, so I had a hard time relating.

"When did you decide to go against what they had planned for you?" I asked.

"Before I went to college. I mean, that's when I decided,

but it took me a while to actually tell them that. My mother cried."

I gaped.

"She cried?" I couldn't picture Laina crying about anything.

"Yup. And my dad was silent. My dad is almost never silent." That was true as far as I'd seen.

"Wow."

"Yeah, it was bad. And every now and then they like to remind me and give me a little dig about how they'd love it if I would move back. I come and visit at least once a month, but it's not enough for them." I'd had no idea about that. Just a week ago, she'd been my annoying coworker and now she was a whole person with a story, and I wasn't sure how I felt about it.

Strange. Slightly fluttery. Uncomfortable.

"We should probably head back. I have to work the dinner shift." I wished it could just be the two of us for the rest of the day.

"I should probably fold some more napkins to pay for my stay and the car repairs."

"You really don't have to do that."

I waved her off. I wasn't going to argue about that again.

∼

I HEADED to the laundry room when we got back and Laura went to find her mother. Michelle looked in on me on the pretense that she was restocking the linen closet.

"Did you have fun with Laura?" she asked as she played with one of the unfolded napkins.

"Yeah, she showed me the high school and we had lunch." She was totally fishing and being pretty obvious about it.

"Oh," she said, her face falling. She looked disappointed. I wasn't going to say anything outright, not unless she asked me out. Then I'd have to break it to her. I hoped it wouldn't come to that.

"Are you going to play Christmas Charades?" I asked her, since that seemed to be the question of the day.

"Absolutely, I play every year. I hope you're on my team." Her voice got a little breathless and then Laina came back and asked her to head to the front desk because someone was checking in.

"Thanks for all your help," she said, picking up a stack of the freshly folded napkins. I was getting pretty good at it. Maybe this could be a whole new career for me? A side hustle at least.

"You're welcome. It's the least I can do." She gave me a strange look that I couldn't interpret. As if she was really seeing me.

"I'm glad you're here, Colden. And I really hope you stay through Christmas." She took the napkins and left before I could say anything else. No idea what that was about. I went back to folding.

∼

CHRISTMAS CHARADES WAS . . . an experience. I didn't end up up on Laura's team but I did get Dan, Sue, Lillian, Greta, and Antonio and a few of the other relatives on mine. It was a pretty good team, and we were in it to win it.

"Rudolph the red-nosed reindeer!" Sue screamed out.

"Yes!" Dan yelled, and we all clapped. He'd been doing this strange animal-like pantomime and I hadn't been anywhere near a guess. Now it was Laura's turn. My team had to remain silent while hers guessed, which was torture if you knew the answer and couldn't do anything about it.

Laura held up one finger.

"First word!" her team yelled out.

She held her hands apart and then pulled them in close. When that didn't get any good guesses, she held up her thumb and forefinger, leaving only a small space between them.

Little, I thought. Little drummer boy. I bet that was it.

Her team was not getting it, so she went to the second word, and pretended to rip a great drum solo. That did it.

Then it was my turn.

I read the card. *It's A Wonderful Life*. Fucking great. How was I supposed to do that? I had a few seconds of panic thinking before I came up with an idea that I hoped would work.

I stood up in front of the group and held up a hand and pretended to shake it, as if I was ringing a bell, then flapped my arms as if they were wings. I was met with blank stares for a minute, and then I got a ton of off-the-wall guesses. At one point, I glanced at Laura and saw her mouthing "It's A Wonderful Life." She got it.

"Oh, it's the movie with Gregory Peck! And he's dead but not! Donna Reed's in it too," Dan said.

"No, it's not Gregory Peck, it's Jimmy Stewart," Lillian said. "Get your actors right."

The clock was ticking down and this was ridiculous.

"It's A Wonderful Life!" Sue finally yelled.

"Yes!" I said. There had only been seconds to spare.

In the end, we did lose, and I could tell Laura was going to gloat about it for a long time.

"So sorry that you weren't good enough," she said, as we hung out in the dining room. There were still a few people hanging out and having tea or coffee and there was a warm feeling that settled in my chest. Laura had her feet propped up on a chair and I had my legs crossed on mine. Guess there really was something to that myth that gays couldn't sit in chairs properly.

"Whatever. It's cute that you care so much. Guess you come by your competitiveness honestly." It also seemed to be genetic. I'd never seen adults get so up in arms about a game of charades before. There was no blood, but it was close.

"I do. It's in the Sterling blood." She sighed and closed her eyes, leaning back in the chair.

"Are you going to stay?"

"I mean, I might as well. I still feel like a mooch, but I don't know. Going back to my apartment alone would be weird now." There was a ding on my phone and I looked down to find a new email.

"Fucking finally." My refund for the imaginary cottage had come through. I immediately transferred some to pay my credit card bills.

"What's up?" Laura asked.

"Got my money back from the rental service for the cottage that wasn't. That's a relief." Huge relief. I almost wanted to get up and do a little dance.

"We should have a drink to celebrate," Laura said, popping to her feet.

"Okay?" I said. I wondered if it was more of that eggnog. Man, that had been intense.

Laura came back a few minutes later with two mugs of liquid.

"Mulled wine. It's the best when it's warmed up." She handed the cup to me and I inhaled the scents of cinnamon and cloves and other warm, spicy things.

I sipped and sighed in relief. This was exactly what I'd needed.

"Do you take requests?" I asked, nodding at the piano.

"For you I could," she said, and we both walked over to the piano. She sat down and I hesitated for a moment before sitting on the bench beside her.

"Do you have enough room?" I asked. She tended to get so

physical with her playing that I didn't know if she was going to knock me out if she got really into it.

"No, you're fine," she said, her voice soft. "What would you like?"

I couldn't stop staring at her mouth, which was slightly red from the wine. Had I ever noticed her lips before? They really were perfectly shaped. I'd heard the phrase "Cupid's bow" before, but I'd never known what it meant until now.

"Huh?" I said, remembering that she'd just asked me something.

"What song would you like?" she said, clearing her throat a little and putting her fingers on the keys.

"Oh, uh, I don't know."

"What's your favorite Christmas song?" she asked, and I had to tear my gaze away from her lips.

"*I'll Be Home For Christmas*," I said. "I know it's supposed to be heartwarming, but the origin story is really sad. I don't know. It makes me feel happy and sad at the same time."

"I get that," Laura said, playing a little riff before starting in on the song. Incredible how she could just . . . play. I was completely in awe of her.

As I sat and listened to her play, the melody and melancholy wistfulness of the song wrapped around me and tears came to my eyes. How embarrassing. I tried to wipe them away, but Laura didn't seem to notice.

When she finished, she opened her eyes and looked at me.

"Are you okay?" I was still trying to stop crying and losing.

"Yeah, I'm fine." I sniffed and wished every piano came with a box of tissues.

"It's okay," she said, using her sleeve to wipe my cheeks. I wanted to tell her to stop, but I didn't.

Laura held her hand to my face and then there was a crash in the dining room that made us jump apart as if we'd been caught doing something illicit.

"I should go see what that was." She got up and stumbled a little before going to check on what hijinks her family was up to. I sat glued to the bench, unable to move.

"I should go to bed," I said aloud to no one. Laura hadn't come back from the dining room and I peeked my head in and saw her sitting with Lillian and laughing about something while Minnie lay asleep at their feet. Seemed like a good time to make my exit.

I went upstairs to my room and closed the door with a sigh. I wished I hadn't left the rest of my wine downstairs, but I wasn't going back to get it.

Giving up on that, I put on a robe and grabbed one of my books to pass the time until sleep. A soft knock at the door startled me.

It was Laura.

"You left this downstairs, and I topped it off." She held the mug out to me. Steam from the warm wine curled into the air.

"Thank you," I said. More words were needed, but I didn't know how to choose the right ones.

"Goodnight?" Laura said. It sounded like a question.

"Goodnight," I said, making a definitive statement. My insides were all twisted and tangled and I needed to sit with the wine and a book and come back to myself.

"Bye," she said, as if disappointed.

"Bye," I said, slowly closing the door. The click of the lock was loud in my ears.

Chapter Seven

My time at The Sterling Inn had taken on a strange rhythm. I slept soundly and had breakfast, usually with Lillian and Minnie and several other members of the family. I hung out with them, sometimes talking, sometimes reading, sometimes watching movies that were projected on a screen in the dining room. Afternoons were for getting coffee and walking outside or driving to town and visiting the tiny shops that sold everything from stuffed lobsters to tacky bumper stickers to Maine maple candy.

Evenings were for dinner and then the ridiculous group activities. Later, I'd hang with Laura as she played the piano, or we'd just talk. I'd go up to bed early and read with a cup of tea.

Things with Laura were . . . weird. Really weird. I kept catching her looking at me and then she'd look away and I swear she was blushing. I got used to seeing her in the waitress outfit with her glasses on after her eyes got too dry from wearing contacts. I got used to her laughing with her cousins and teasing her dad and goofing with her great-grandmother. I even got used to seeing a giant pig running around.

I made the decision before I told them that I was going to

stay. In fact, every time I got up the courage to say it, I backed off and couldn't say the words. So I just hung around. No one asked me if I was going to leave. They just kept including me as if I was one of them.

One night I was reading late because my book was gay and good, when I heard a ruckus in the hallway. At first I thought that Minnie had gotten loose again, so I ignored it. Minnie was one smart pig and she managed to get through doors more than once already. Nothing unusual.

Then I heard more voices and there was a loud knock at the door. I put on my robe and went to see what was happening and found a breathless Michelle.

"Hey, were you sleeping?"

I shook my head.

"Sorry, but there's been a fire at a home up the road and the family needs somewhere to stay. They had a ton of relatives staying with them, so there's more than a dozen people. Laina is putting them up here. Would you be okay staying at the main house?" I couldn't process what was happening and before I could say anything, there was Laina.

"Oh, Colden, I'm glad I caught you. Would you mind bunking with Laura for the night? We just have this poor family and they have a new baby and two other kids and they need the suite." So many things were happening so fast.

I blinked a few times and then since everyone seemed to be waiting for me to answer, so I said, "yeah, sure" before I could process what I was agreeing to.

Less than an hour later, me and one of my suitcases were walking the path between the inn and the house next door. I wasn't sure if I should knock, but the door swung open before I could raise my hand.

Laura.

"Hey, uh, I guess we're sharing a room?" Laura nodded, her mouth pressed into a hard line.

"Come on in." I tried not to feel like an intruder, but I did.

"Listen, I can, um, go sleep on the couch or something." The house was big and beautifully decorated, except where the inn was more dark wood and warm tones, this place was light and airy, but still cozy.

"No, you can stay in my room. I have a big bed." I swallowed hard. This evening had taken quite a turn.

"No, it's fine, I'll stay on the couch." There was no way I was going to sleep in her bed tonight. No way.

"Suit yourself," she said.

Laura gave me a tour of the house, which had four large bedrooms, but all of them were occupied, except for Laura's. Well, it was occupied by her.

"There's no room for me at the inn," I said, pouting. Laura laughed at my joke.

"I swear, if a little boy with a drum, and three wise dudes show up, I'm going to freak out," she said.

"I'm pretty sure I'm not the second coming. But you never know." It was too early for me to go to bed, and Laura didn't seem inclined that way either.

"You want to watch a movie or something?" she asked, and I figured I didn't have anything else to do.

"Sure."

"Have you ever seen *White Christmas*?"

I hadn't.

"Okay, that's what we're watching. I watch this movie all the time when I feel sad. No matter what time of year it is." A comfort movie. I had many, along with comfort books. It wasn't lost on me that this was a special thing for Laura to share with me. I appreciated it.

"Snacks?" she asked.

"Always," I said. "Do you need any help?"

"No, I can handle it." The kitchen and the living room were open to each other, so I could see her getting things from the fridge and arranging items on what looked like a wooden board. How fancy.

"Are you making charcuterie?" I yelled, leaning over the back of the couch. It was more interesting to watch her than anything on the TV.

"Maybe," she said, smiling at me.

"Can I watch?" I asked.

"You want to watch?" I hopped over the back of the couch and walked into the kitchen.

"Oh, wow," I said when I saw what she'd done. This wasn't a cheese and cracker plate. No, she had olives and prosciutto and several kinds of cheeses and fancy nuts and strawberries.

"Can I take a picture of it?" I asked, and she gave me a look as if I was being ridiculous. "It's beautiful. Do you ever do anything halfway? I feel like everything you do is perfect." That was kind of an understatement.

"I'm not perfect, Colden," she said. There it was again. The way she said my name. Laura kept her eyes on the charcuterie plate, arranging things and moving them around, even though it was basically done.

"Can we eat it now?" I asked, and she glanced up.

"Okay," she said. I made sure to take a picture with my phone before she brought it over to the coffee table, grabbed a few seltzer waters, and then put the movie on.

I went for the snacks immediately.

"Try the truffle goat cheese on that cracker," Laura said, pointing to one of the cheeses. This was fancier cheese than I'd eaten in a long time. It was nothing but high class at Chez Sterling.

I cut some of the crumbly cheese and put it on one of the crackers before popping the whole thing in my mouth.

"Oh my god," I said, my eyes almost rolling back in my head. The cheese was rich and had ribbons of black truffle running through it, giving it a delicious earthy taste that was just unbelievable.

"I want to eat this every single day for the rest of my life," I said.

"It's from a local farm, actually. We can go there while you're here if you want. You can pet the goats and everything." That was something I definitely had to do before going back to the city.

I settled back on the couch with my snack and Laura pulled a soft woven blanket off the arm of a nearby chair.

"Blanket? We always watch movies with blankets, so I can't relax and watch one without being covered up, even in the summer." I agreed and she spread the blanket over both of us. I'd inadvertently sat in the middle of the couch, instead of on the other end away from her. I'd wanted to be close to the snacks, but it turned out I was close to Laura. It worked for blanket sharing, but it was awkward for just about everything else.

Her hand brushed mine as she reached for her seltzer water, and I had to be careful my leg didn't touch hers when I moved it.

"Dear god, her waist is small," I said about one of the two female actresses staring in the movie.

"Yeah, she had an eating disorder. Really sad. She made them let her cover her neck the whole movie because she was dealing with premature aging. Pretty tragic." Not the kind of thing you wanted to be thinking about during a heartwarming film, but Hollywood had been a brutal place.

I hadn't watched an old-school musical in a long time, and it gave me the same feeling as mulled wine did.

"I don't normally watch Christmas movies," I confessed. "They just make me sad and bitter usually, but this one isn't bad." It was less about the holiday and more about the people and the singing and dancing.

Laura sighed next to me, but it was a contented sigh. I looked at her out of the corner of my eye. She had a slight smile on her face as she watched the movie.

She really was beautiful. I mean, I always knew that, but it was different somehow. Her beauty was less cold now. Less "model in a magazine" and more "woman you passed on the street that was so pretty your knees buckled."

I had to stop staring at her, but it was mesmerizing, watching the light from the TV dance across her face. I sipped my seltzer and choked.

"Are you okay?"

I wheezed and she patted me on the back.

"Yeah, I'm fine." I'd almost died from choking on seltzer water because I'd been too busy staring at her to pay attention to drinking. What a pathetic way to die that would have been.

Embarrassed, I kept my eyes on the movie for the rest of the time. She got up about halfway through and paused it.

"I'll be right back." She went to the bathroom and I waited for her to return. I flipped through my phone and had an idea. I went online and searched for it. I put the item in my cart and then looked up the address for the Sterling Inn before completing the purchase. It would be here before Christmas.

Laura got back under the blanket with me and the return of her warmth was both cozy and disconcerting. She started the movie again and we watched all the way through.

"Did you cry?" she asked, as I tried to wipe my wet eyes without attracting notice.

"No," I said through sniffles.

"It's okay, it makes me cry too," she said, wiping one last tear. Of course she was a pretty crier. I turned into a puffy, blotchy, snotty mess, but Laura cried like she was in a movie.

"That was really good," I said. "I'm sorry I haven't seen it before."

"We watch it every Christmas, but not until Christmas Eve.

I hope you're around for that. We go all out." They hadn't gone all out yet? This was the most extreme Christmas I'd ever seen.

"I might regret asking this, but what do you do on Christmas Eve?"

Laura smiled slowly.

"We do Christmas Trivia, which is always ridiculous, we have Christmas dinner, which is always lobster, we watch *White Christmas* and then we each get to open one present, which is always the same thing." Her eyes twinkled.

"What is it?" I asked, and then braced for the answer.

"Christmas pajamas. There's a theme every year and we all get pajamas. Then comes the fashion show. There's a runway. There are judges. There's music and lots of heckling. After that is everyone writing a letter to Santa, putting out cookies and milk, and carrots for the reindeer, and then everyone goes to bed. You game for that?"

That was so many things happening. Even when I'd celebrated with Dad, we'd never done anything super elaborate. It had always been kind of lowkey. I'd always been jealous of the kids with tons of siblings and grandparents and so forth who had these big marathon celebrations, sometimes at multiple houses.

"I don't know, am I?" I asked.

"I think you can handle it. And if not, there's always lots of eggnog to get you through." Good point.

"We'll see," I said. I didn't want to commit to anything.

With the movie over, Laura got up and put away everything from the charcuterie extravaganza and then brought me some more blankets and pillows for the couch.

"Um, do you want to go to bed?" she asked, as she wiped down the sink in the kitchen.

"Do you?" I'd do whatever she was doing. I didn't want to be a burden.

"Not really. This is early for me." Another night owl. I guess I had known that since I got work emails from her past eleven, but it was still a relief to hear it.

"Do you want to just read?" she asked, and I almost melted to the floor in relief.

"Yes, I do." I fished one of my books out of my suitcase and she grabbed one from her room.

"Oh, you got an advanced copy of that?"

It was a book I'd been dying to get my hands on, but didn't know how to get.

"Uh, yeah. I may or may not have stolen it from work." The guilt on her face was so cute.

"Are you serious?" I asked. "I've been whining online for a copy for weeks and you just had one? How dare you." I reached to snatch the book out of her hands, but she stepped back.

"Oh, I will fight you," she said, pointing at me with the hand that wasn't holding the book. "Plus, I'm taller than you."

She had me there. But I also had my ways.

"Just you wait, Laura Sterling. Just you wait. I can be patient when I want something. I'll just bide my time." I stepped back and pretended that I wasn't interested in the book anymore, but her eyes narrowed.

"I don't trust you," she said.

"Likewise."

With no further drama, we ended up on the couch again, this time on opposite ends, each with a paperback in our hands.

The only sound in the house was the soft rumble of voices in the other rooms, the grind of the refrigerator, and the tick of a clock in the corner.

Laura was a fast reader, I soon discovered. Her pages turned more rapidly than mine did, partially due to the fact that I was watching her read, and she was actually doing the reading.

"Are you reading or watching me read?" she asked, without even looking up as she turned a page.

"I'm doing a bit of both," I said. It wasn't that my book was boring, it was that Laura was interesting.

"Is there a reason?" She still wasn't looking up from the book. Guess she was multitasking.

"You read really fast. I'm learning what I'm up against at the office." I'd learned a whole lot more in these few days with her than I'd learned in a year of working with her. To be fair, I had done whatever I could to ignore her when we were at work and block out anything about her.

"I guess I read fast." Page turn. "But you could be reading if you weren't focusing on me. Eyes on your own page, Colden." I narrowed my eyes. I didn't like her telling me what to do.

I wanted to make a snarky remark, but I couldn't think of one, so I went back to my book and let myself get lost in the story and stopped thinking about Laura. At least for the most part. She was still there, hovering on the edge of my awareness. She was a distracting person to read near.

I didn't know how much time had passed, but she eventually put a bookmark in between the pages and looked up at me.

"I think I'm done for the night. How about you?"

I was just about to answer her when someone came through the front door.

It was Griffin and one of the other teen cousins who I couldn't remember the name of because they all looked the same.

"Hey, can we crash on the couch? We lost our rooms."

I looked at Laura and she looked back. My only options were to sleep on the floor or to crash with Laura. As much as I didn't want to share a room with Laura, I hated the idea of sleeping on the floor more.

"Yeah, that's fine," I said. "Guess I'm sharing with you after all."

Laura got her cousins set up on the couch and I followed her up to her room.

I wasn't ready to go to bed yet. Bed meant sharing a very intimate space with Laura. I was never going to be ready for that.

"Yeah, sounds good," I said instead. She folded the blanket again and I followed her to her room. She had an attached bathroom, which was a blessing. Laura grabbed some clothes and went to the bathroom to change and brush her teeth.

She came back wearing silky pants and a tank that didn't leave much to the imagination. I'd never seen her in pajamas before. I gulped and rushed to the bathroom so I wouldn't get accused of staring again.

Unlike Laura, I didn't have sexy pajamas. I had flannel shorts and a t-shirt that had a dancing piece of pizza on it. Super sexy.

Wait, why did I care if my sleepwear was sexy? The only one who was going to see it was Laura, and I didn't care about being sexy in front of Laura.

I brushed my teeth more carefully than I had in my life. I brushed as if I was going to straight to a dentist who would murder me if my teeth weren't pristine. Mostly I was avoiding going back into the bedroom.

It was pretty much what I'd expected: soft colors, pops of blue and yellow here and there, and everything was arranged just so. Her pillows even had that little divot in the middle that people who put their homes in magazines did.

Her bathroom was also massive, and had a tub and a walk-in shower. I briefly considered asking if I could use it, but that would be weird. I didn't need to use Laura's shower.

She sat in one of the chairs in a corner of the room where

she'd made a little seating area. My eyes went from her to the bed. There it was. The bed we would share.

"If you want, I can put some blankets on the floor," she said.

"No, that's not necessary. We can share." I'd shared a bed platonically with friends many times before. I guess this was part of our budding friendship. I had agreed to try to be friends with her, so I guess this was one step forward in that direction.

"Are you sure?" she asked. I glanced from the bed to her. One of her knees jiggled up and down. Was she nervous?

"Yeah," I said. "Unless you aren't? I swear, I can crash on the couch. It's fine. I've done it before."

"No, I'm not going to make you do that. Uh, what side do you want?" There were nightstands on either side of the bed, along with a sweet little lamp. It was easy to see which side was Laura's. There was a glasses case, a book, and a bottle of pills.

"I'll take the left," I said, moving toward the side that wasn't hers.

"Okay," she said, walking around the other side.

I got in the crisp sheets and they smelled sharp and clean. The bed dipped as Laura got in, knocked back a few pills and swallowed some water.

I'd brought my before-bed book with me and she retrieved hers. It was just like being on the couch, but it was completely different.

Our warmth mingled under the blankets and I sunk back on her pillows. They were fluffy and numerous. I made a note to buy myself some nice pillows when I got back. I had the money for them now.

Laura pulled her legs up and rested her book on them.

She was too distracting again.

"What are you reading?" She held it up so I could read the title.

"Nice," I said. It was one I'd already read. She didn't seem interested in mine, but I turned it around so she could see anyway.

"Oh, I love that one. I've read it like three times."

"This is my second time through. I don't like to read new books when I'm trying to go to sleep. I did that too many times, and regretted it when I couldn't get up for work in the morning." Ironic that I couldn't go to my job of reading books because I'd stayed up too late reading books.

"Been there done that, have the t-shirt to prove it," she said, and I laughed. Our eyes met and I had to remind myself to breathe. She smiled shyly and I had to tear myself away and focus on the pages of my book, but the words swam in front of my eyes as if I'd had too much eggnog.

Laura let out that little sigh and I had the strangest feeling in my body. I couldn't even put my finger on it, but I was utterly and completely comfortable. Usually it took me forever to feel sleepy, but tonight it was as if I'd taken a warm bath, or I'd gone to a long yoga class.

Laura shifted and then I was wide awake again, but still comfortable.

I set my book down and turned to Laura.

"Do you mind if I go to bed?"

"Not at all. Will the light bother you?"

I shook my head. When I was alone I sometimes slept with the TV on, so a little lamplight wasn't too intense.

I curled on my side, my back to her.

"Goodnight," I said. "And thank you. For taking me in."

"You're welcome. Goodnight, Colden." I closed my eyes and sunk into the mattress. Maybe I should invest in a new one as well. Laura's was heaven.

The room was so quiet. The loudest sound was when Laura turned a page. She was reading fast again.

I tried to sleep, but it had run away from me again, so

annoying. Not wanting to disturb her by moving too much, I stayed where I was. Somehow, my arm started to fall asleep, so I tried to shift and wake it up, but nothing was working. I turned slowly onto my other side, still pretending I was asleep, or at least close to sleep.

Now I faced Laura, and could see adn feel her every little movement. She read for a while longer and then set the book aside and the light went out. Laura wiggled down under the blankets and stayed on her back. I was always a side sleeper, and I'd always been envious of back sleepers. It seemed so easy.

Just as I started to drift a little, she turned on her side, and we were facing each other. I knew that if I opened my eyes, her face would be right there. Her breath moved my hair, but she didn't breathe directly on me. She probably thought I was asleep, but I was even further from sleep now.

Laura was right there and I was right here and we were in the same bed.

What a situation to find myself in.

Something touched my hair and I stopped breathing for a second. I didn't know what to do, but I couldn't keep my eyes closed anymore.

Chapter Eight

Laura was touching my hair and Laura was definitely awake. I opened my eyes to find her staring at me.

"Oh," she said in a whisper. "I thought you were asleep."

"Nope," I said. "I've been awake the whole time."

"Oh," she repeated. "I'm sorry." She pulled her hand back and closed her eyes. I acted without thinking.

"Hey," I said, touching her cheek. Her eyes popped open.

"It's okay." The darkness made things different. The darkness changed everything.

"Is it?" she asked.

"Yes," I said.

I stroked the side of her face, putting some of her hair behind her ear. She almost always wore her hair down and I had never noticed that her ears stuck out just a little bit. Perfectly adorable.

Laura's breath stuttered and I could feel her entire body shaking.

"It's okay." I stopped touching her and she reached out again, but she did something I wasn't expecting. She wrapped her hand around the back of my neck and drew my face closer to hers.

There was just enough light to see the outline of her face.

Laura was going to kiss me and I was going to let her. No, I wasn't just going to let her. I was going to kiss her back.

Just before the moment of no return, she paused and our eyes locked. She gave me a chance to pull back. To say no. To put on the brakes. To stop the whole thing.

I didn't want to stop. It had been so long since I'd been close to anyone and my skin craved touch. I craved closeness, even if it was just for tonight. Even if it was just for this moment.

In fact, I was the one who pressed my lips to Laura's. Hers were trembling so much, that I reached out to steady her with both hands on her shoulders.

The shock of the kiss hit me hard. For a second, I had to remember how to kiss. It had been a while since I'd done any serious kissing. For a moment, we were just two people touching our lips together, nothing more. Then a switch flicked and the kiss turned on.

Laura's fingers gripped my neck and pulled me closer and before I knew what was happening, my entire body was up against Laura's and my fingers tugged her hair and I was kissing her in a hopeless and desperate way as if it was my first and last kiss and I had to give it everything or die.

I almost did feel like I was going to die. I couldn't breathe, I couldn't think, I could only feel the heat between us, the electric energy.

Her mouth was raw and relentless, asking for more and taking it from me. I fought back and it was almost a battle for who wanted the other one more.

There was no time to stop and think about the implications of this kiss. The time for that would come later. There was only now.

Laura made a little whimpering noise in her throat and it was so cute, I almost smiled. If my mouth hadn't been busy making out with her, I might have.

I gasped and fumbled and slipped my tongue between her lips and learned that Laura was extremely good at yet something else.

Damn, this girl could kiss. Holy shit. Either she'd had a lot of practice, or she was naturally gifted or both.

While we kissed, my hands went exploring. I traced her shoulders, bare except for the insignificant straps of the tank. It would be so easy to get rid of those straps and have full access to touch her perfect skin. I definitely hadn't had much experience with touching her like this. I hadn't had much experience with touching her at all. I'd always avoided it and now I was starting to see why.

I wanted her. I wanted Laura, and this feeing hadn't come upon me just in this moment. No, I'd wanted her for a while. No idea when it had started, but it was here and it was overwhelming.

I felt her pulling away from me and internally I screamed.

"Hey," she said, and my eyes snapped open. There she was, right there in front of me with kiss-swollen lips. I'd been kissing those lips. The world tilted on its axis and even though I was lying down, I felt like I was falling.

"Hey," I said back to her.

"I can't believe this is happening." Her fingers twirled pieces of my hair and I kept waiting for my better judgment to take over and for me to realize what an absolutely terrible idea this was, but it wasn't happening. No, I just wanted to kiss her more. And more. And more.

There were other things I wanted as well. Things I wasn't even going to name.

"Are you okay?"

I hadn't spoken and didn't trust myself. Instead, I kissed her again. I felt a momentary protest, as if she wanted to talk this out, but then she melted into me and I didn't have to answer any more questions for a little while. That was safer. That was easier.

Our tongues met again and twirled in a slow dance of give and take. My hands continued their exploration of her upper body, and I got a little reckless, reaching for her to come closer.

Laura made a frustrated sound in her throat and then threw off the covers.

"Sorry, I'm sweating my ass off under here." I'd been too focused on the kissing that I hadn't noticed that I'd heated up as well. The air chilled me for a brief second, but then I reached for her again.

"Come here," she said, laying on her back. Oh, this changed things. I scooted closer and slowly placed my body atop hers.

"You can touch me, Colden. I'm not going to break." I'd been sort of hovering, not wanting to put my full weight on her.

"Okay," I said, letting myself relax onto her. There were so many parts of our bodies touching. It overloaded my brain for a second. Then she did something that made me black out. She wrapped her legs and arms around me and this time, she kissed me.

I'd never quite appreciated how long and luscious her legs were, but I fully enjoyed them now. Her fingernails dug into my skin and it was like she flipped a switch in my brain and then things turned a little feral.

I pulled her lip between my teeth and dug my hands into her shoulders and drove my hips into hers repeatedly. Was this what she wanted? I was going to give it to her. That only seemed to make her want more.

She yanked at my clothes and I pulled at hers and there was a battle for a few moments to see who was going to get the other one's top off first. Finally, she broke the kiss with a laugh.

"We can both get our shirts off, but we can't do it at the same time. Let's get yours off first." My eyes narrowed as I looked down at her, chest heaving. The blood pounded like a drum in my ears.

"Don't tell me what to do," I said.

"You're the one on top. It's easier for you to get yours off first," she pointed out.

"Your logic has no place here," I said, but she was right. "Ugh, fine. If you wanna see my tits, fine." I pulled my shirt over my head and made a little presentation motion with my hands.

"You'd better love them. I grew them myself."

Her eyes got wide and she swallowed audibly.

"They're perfect," she said in a hushed voice.

"These old things? You're so sweet." I looked down and didn't think much of them, but Laura looked at me as if she'd never seen boobs before and it was pretty flattering.

"Can I touch you?" she asked.

"Yeah, knock yourself out." I'd never really cared much about having my chest touched, but if she wanted to go for it, I wasn't going to stop her.

The second her fingers brushed my nipples, I moaned. So much for not caring about having those touched. Laura cupped my breasts and rubbed them, focusing on my nipples, giving them plenty of attention. They hardened into needy peaks and I arched into her, wanting more.

She grew bolder, testing a little pinch with each nipple and then backing off to watch them harden even more.

"Yes, please," I said. "You can go harder." Apparently I liked nipple pinching, who knew?

I wasn't thinking about her getting her shirt off. I wasn't thinking about anything but the feeling of her teasing and taunting me with her fingers. And then she sat up and put her mouth on me and I almost passed out.

Had my nipples gained sensitivity in the past five minutes? She bit down on one hard enough to make me moan even louder.

"Shhh," she said, licking the same nipple with her tongue. "My parents are sleeping down the hall."

My eyes flew open. Well, shit.

"I'm not good at being quiet, Laura," I said. "You should probably know that."

"Well, you're going to have to try," she said matter-of-factly as she took my other nipple into her mouth, sucking on it briefly before biting that one.

I clamped my hand over my mouth. This was not going to be easy.

"Mmm, maybe we should switch? At least I know how to be quiet." I opened my mouth and glared at her, but also I wanted to see her without her shirt on, so I swung my leg over her and flopped back on the bed.

Laura straddled my legs with hers and this was a whole new angle to appreciate her. She pulled her tank over her head and as much as I loved having her biting my nipples, this was better.

"Fucking hell," I said. Her chest was generous in the best way, falling heavy and round. I could fill my hands with them and I wanted to.

"What's this?" I asked, tracing a horizontal scar on her stomach.

"Appendix. It burst when I was in high school during assembly. It was all very dramatic." I also saw a dot above her belly button that signified that she might have had it pierced at one time. I had learned so many things about Laura in these few seconds. I wonder what other secrets her body held that I would get to unwrap. Christmas was coming early for me.

I took my time studying her, counting each freckle and scar before I turned my full attention to her incredible tits. I did what I wanted and filled my hands with them. She threw her head back and made a quiet sound of pleasure. I hoped that if she didn't have to be quiet, the sound would have normally been louder. I didn't want to mess around, so I brought my mouth to first one of her boobs and then the other. I kissed and sucked on the skin until it turned red and I hoped I left a mark. I wanted her to look at herself tomorrow and know that I'd been here. I wanted her to remember this.

I didn't stop until her boobs were peppered with red marks and I'd teased her so thoroughly she'd started begging in a hoarse whisper. Who ever thought that the sound I would most want to hear was Laura pleading with me? I loved it.

"You're a monster," she said as I ran my hand down her stomach to cup her between her legs.

"I thought I was the Grinch?" My heart was definitely too small, but only because it had been broken into multiple pieces and parts had been shattered that would never get put back together.

"I don't know who you are but, oh my god." I pressed the heel of my hand against her and she arched back again.

"I'm not god either," I said. "But I do want more of you." Laura looked at me with lust-glazed eyes.

"Huh?" she said.

"Get on your back, baby." The endearment fell from my lips so naturally that I didn't know why I hadn't been calling her that this entire time.

Laura did what I asked, and I was back on top. I didn't mind being in control like this as I shimmied her shorts and undies down her legs. I was sure her underwear was cute and I'd probably want to see her in it later, but right now I was only concerned about what was underneath.

I got rid of the rest of her clothes and then there she was, in all her glory, and I had to take a moment to thank whatever deity saw fit to let me have this moment.

"You're stunning," I said. I'd never seen anyone so perfect. I looked up to her face and found her with red cheeks.

"What is it?"

"It's embarrassing."

"What is?"

"Being naked. It's so weird. I just . . . all I can think about are the parts I don't like about myself." I scanned her up and down.

"I'm sorry, I don't see any parts not to like. You're completely and totally gorgeous." Her cheeks got even more red.

"Thanks. It's easier to believe that when you say it."

"You know me, I don't bullshit. I tell the truth because my face always betrays the lie."

"I know," she said, nodding. "I just had an ex who was really critical during sex and it kind of messed me up." Firstly, I wanted to find that ex and stab them, and second, I was going to do my best to make her feel beautiful while she was with me.

"I know how you feel. Sometimes my body isn't what I want it to be, or what I see in my head." I didn't want to drag the mood down with dysphoria, but I could understand what she was talking about.

"But I'm not going to talk about that, or think about that, because I'm going to distract you so thoroughly, you won't be thinking about anything else." I gave her a wicked smile and her eyes went wide again.

"And how are you going to do that?" she asked.

"Just you wait."

I tried to project a whole lot more confidence than I felt, but honestly, eating pussy wasn't rocket surgery. I just had to listen to her responses and try everything in my bag of tricks.

I'd thoroughly loved on her tits, so I explored other areas

including her neck, her collarbone, her bellybutton, her calves, her knees. I tasted and touched as much of her skin as I could, paying extra attention to any areas that made her writhe and beg. I'd never been with someone who went wild when I kissed the side of their hips, but there was a first for everything.

She pleaded and begged and fussed and thrashed until I stroked her just where she'd asked me to and she sighed in relief. I guess I wasn't the only one who was a little wound up.

I licked one of my fingers before slowly entering her. She thrust her hips into my hand and I could tell that one finger was good, but two fingers was better for her, so I quickly added a second, thrusting and curling my fingers the way she wanted and needed. Wanting to completely blow her mind, I shifted my weight and added my tongue into the mix and that pushed her over the edge.

I had to reach up and clamp the hand that wasn't helping prolong her climax onto her mouth so she wouldn't make so much noise. Now who was the one who couldn't be quiet?

Her tremors quieted and she gasped. I raised my head and realized it would have been a good idea to put my hair up before we started this whole thing, but there was no going back now.

"Wow," Laura said, looking down at me and pushing my damp hair out of my face. I was probably a complete mess, but she was happy and that was all I cared about at the moment.

"That was incredible."

"Why thank you. Do you need a minute or are you ready to go again?" Her eyes popped open.

"Again? Don't you want to have a turn?"

"Only when I'm done with you."

"When will you be done with me?"

"I'm not sure yet." I smiled and stroked her again. "I'm just getting started."

∽

I MADE her come three more times and she begged me to stop. I wiped my face on her sheets and climbed up to lay next to her. I still had my shorts on for some reason.

"I think I'm dead," she said, staring at the ceiling. Her whole body was flushed and glistening with sweat. Sexy as fuck, and the best part was the knowledge that I was responsible for her looking that way.

"How is your hair still perfect?" I asked.

"It's not," she said, running her hands through her hair as it fell perfectly back on the pillow.

She turned on her side and smiled at me. My broken heart rattled in my chest a little.

"I had no idea this was going to happen. I had no idea you were going to happen."

"It's not like this was my grand plan. Sometimes shit happens and you go with it." I'd abandoned the idea that "everything happens for a reason" shortly after I understood that not everyone's mother left them. There was no grand plan. There was just life.

"I'm not going to lie, I've had the biggest fucking crush on you since we started working."

"Are you fucking serious?" This was news to me. "You couldn't stand me. The feeling was mutual." Hadn't it been?

"I was upset that you were so distracting. Do you know how hard it's been sitting in the same office and trying to work near you for the past year?" I gaped at her. With those few words, Laura had turned everything I thought was right upside down.

"So you were so annoying because you liked me? Did you steal work because you liked me?" Weird way to show it, if true.

"If you want to call it annoying. I like to think of it as

awkward work flirting. But I wasn't going to sacrifice my crush for getting ahead at work so . . ." she trailed off and shrugged.

"You are possibly one of the most frustrating people I have ever met, Laura Sterling. But you're sexy as hell, so it all evens out." I laughed and she hit me lightly on the shoulder.

"Rude. Maybe I won't fuck you now." I needed to come so bad that it felt like my junk was pressing on my brain, making it hard to think.

"Please fuck me?" I asked. "Ugh, that sounded so needy. But it's true. Please?" A seductive smile spread on her lips and she put her hand on my shoulder to pin me to the bed.

"Let's see what we can do for you, shall we?" Without another word, she yanked off my shorts and undies, just as I'd done for her.

"Is there anything you absolutely don't want?" she asked, which made me stop for a second.

"I mean, yeah. Please don't like, spit on me and call me a whore. Not a fan. But I mean, I'll let you know if you're going in the wrong direction." She ran her hands between my boobs.

"I want to make you feel like you made me feel." Her fingers trembled just a little and she looked up at me.

She was nervous.

"Hey, baby, it's okay. Just follow your instincts." I touched her face and pointed to my junk. "You can always start here. It's a very good place to start."

That made her laugh and kiss my mouth. She didn't start with my junk. No, she started with my neck. Laura kissed and scraped my skin with her teeth and sucked and if I'd had any blood left in my brain to form a thought, I would have realized tomorrow I'd have an impressive set of hickies.

Laura kissed my body like she did everything else: with determined precision. She cut right to the places that drove me wild and made me squirm and let out incoherent sounds that I had to try and muffle so her parents wouldn't hear. This hadn't been the ideal location for our first encounter. By the time she headed toward my junk with her hands, my entire body was vibrating with need and desire.

Before I knew what was happening, she had me on my side facing her. Our mouths touched, and she wiggled her clever fingers near where I wanted her.

"Tease," I said into her mouth.

"I'm just getting warmed up." She cupped me and I moaned, but she swallowed the sound.

There was a lot more moaning as she slid first one, and then a second finger inside me. The angle was perfect for her to hit everything right. My hips started moving of their own free will, demanding more, begging for release.

I clamped my thighs together on her hand and rode out my release against her as she kissed me gently. Wave after wave hit me, robbing me of breath as stars exploded behind my closed eyelids. Laura teased every last drop of pleasure from me and left me tingling in the aftermath.

My eyes opened slowly, and she was right there.

"You're so beautiful," she said, kissing the tip of my nose. "I'm going to make you pay for earlier," she whispered into my ear before nipping my earlobe, causing me to jump.

"No, don't, stop," I said as a weak and fake protest.

"Are you ready?" she asked.

I would never be ready for Laura Sterling.

∼

SHE MADE me come as many times as I'd made her, even though it took a little longer. Desire could be tricky and something that worked five minutes ago might not work in future. If we did this again, I was going to get out my trusty vibrator and really give her a show.

We didn't talk about a next time. Instead we stripped the bed, took a shower to wash off, and then made the bed again.

It was the middle of the fucking night and both of us were exhausted. We didn't bother to put clothes on before getting under the covers again. This time she held me close and I told myself that I didn't need to fuck her again. I'd fucked her enough for one night.

Laura sighed that happy sigh again, and I nestled into her chest and closed my eyes, at last, to sleep.

Chapter Nine

When I woke a few hours later, sunlight streamed through a crack in the curtains and I took in the aftermath of the night. My hair was an utter disaster from being slept on while wet, there were clothes everywhere, and a pile of bedding sat in the corner of the room as if it was judging me.

I turned and found Laura still asleep. Yet again, perfect hair. It wasn't fair, it really wasn't.

A smile softened her face and made her look like a fallen angel. Ugh, I was really losing it. I didn't want to have all these warm and slippery feelings in my chest. I missed the cold indifference.

Had I really ever been indifferent to Laura, though? Not when I thought back. Maybe part of my annoyance was my annoyance at my own attraction to her.

It was too early, and I'd had too little sleep to be thinking about this shit. I needed some distance from the situation, some distance from Laura.

Her eyes opened slowly and she blinked up at me.

"Hey, are you watching me sleep?"

"Uh, no. I mean, I was, but not really? Not in a creepy way. You're just really pretty." She laughed softly.

"Thank you. I think you're really pretty. If that's an okay word to use?"

I nodded.

"But if you ever want to call me handsome, I wouldn't be upset."

"You got it," she said, stretching out. "Ow."

My own body was heavy and stiff. I wanted to lay in bed all day.

"Do you want breakfast?" she asked.

"Yeah, is there any way that we can be normal so your family doesn't know . . . what we did?"

She gave me a look. "Do you really think they don't already know that something is going on?"

Oh. OH.

"I mean, I had some kind of suspicions, but not really. Oh, and I think your cousin has a crush on me, but she hasn't said anything. I mean, I don't want to have to reject her, but if you could maybe drop some hints?"

Laura yawned and said she would.

"Poor Michelle. I keep trying to get her to come out to the city. I have two bedrooms and I would totally let her crash with me while she got on her feet, but she's still too scared to leave the bubble. It's not easy when everything but your own heart is telling you to stay."

"You should tell her that, if you haven't already. I'll talk to her too, but I'll try not to make it into flirting or anything."

Laura narrowed her eyes.

"What?"

"I'm not sure if I trust this not-flirting business. I might need to be nearby just in case."

"Just in case you have to jump in and save me from accidentally flirting?"

"Exactly."

I burst out laughing.

"You're ridiculous."

"You love it," she said, grabbing the pillow from under her head and then hitting me with it. What happened next was my first real pillow fight. Feathers didn't fly around, but we laughed and hit each other and ran around the bedroom and probably made too much noise.

I was laughing so hard that I couldn't breath and collapsed on the floor.

"We're such a cliché right now," I said, when I caught my breath.

"How's that?" she asked, sitting down next to me.

"We're having a naked pillow fight. We're a porn parody right now."

She lay back and put the pillow under her head. I got distracted from thoughts about the pillow fight by her body in the morning light.

"Damn, we should have filmed it and then we could have made some money. Next time?" I hoped she was joking.

She'd closed her eyes, so I couldn't really tell.

"As long as I get to pick my name. I want to have a kickass sexy name."

"Deal," she said, opening her eyes and holding her hand out. "You know I'm joking, right?"

"I hoped you were, but I wasn't sure. I mean, if that's your thing, that's awesome. I just don't know if I could have the courage to do it. Plus, that shit is a lot of work. You have to hustle."

Laura and I lay on the floor and talked about sex work and jobs and money and a whole bunch of other things. Just talking naked on the floor.

"Okay, we should probably put clothes on," she said,

getting to her feet. "And I'm starving. Breakfast?" She held her hand out to me and I let her pull me up to standing.

"Do we have to face your family?"

She took my hand and held it in hers.

"We have three choices: we can stay in this room and starve, we can go to breakfast and pretend nothing happened, or we can go to breakfast and not pretend nothing happened, but I don't know if I really want to get into the dirty details just yet, don't you think?"

"That's a double negative," I said, and she kissed my cheek.

"You're cute. Let's get dressed." We put our clothes on and she took my fingers in hers for a few moments, but let go of my hand just before she opened the door and I felt a profound loss. It was still too early to analyze any of this.

∽

LAINA WAS busy in the laundry room when we walked through the back door of the inn.

"You'll be fine," Laura whispered to me, as she said good morning to her mother. Antonio was already singing in the kitchen as he made omelets and pancakes and sliced fruit. I didn't know how he managed to cook all the food for everyone, but he had it down to a science.

"How was your night last night?" Laina asked, looking from me to Laura and back.

"It was fine," Laura said. "No drama, right?"

"Yeah, fine," I said, feeling my face get hot. It was probably as red as a lobster right now. Why was I so bad at lying?

"Good. Because the family is going to be here through Christmas. How do you feel about sharing a room for a while? I'm so sorry, Colden, but I'm not going to let them be left out in the cold." Of course not.

"No, it's fine, I completely understand. Is there anything we can do?"

Her eyes brightened up.

"I was hoping you would ask that. Can you go get them some clothes and some toys and things for the kids? We're putting together donations, but new items would be great. I have lists of sizes. Can you go after breakfast?"

Laura and I both agreed that we would, and would pick up anything else the families might need. Laina said that a local TV station was also coming to interview the families and her about everything.

"I don't really want to do it, but I'm going to ask for donations, so it's for them." She smoothed her hands on her perfect hair. Like mother, like daughter.

"You'll be fine," Laura said to her mom. "We're going to eat quick and then leave, but text me if you need anything else."

Laura and I said hello to Antonio and he showed me the breakfast menu and asked what I wanted. I was ravenous after the coital gymnastics, so I asked for a three-egg veggie omelet, bacon, potatoes, and a croissant.

"A little hungry?" Laura said in my ear and I kicked her leg to get her to stop saying sexy things in my ear in front of her dad. He was too busy flipping eggs and minding bacon to see at the moment, but I didn't want to take any chances.

When we got into the dining room I saw the increase in unfamiliar faces. The adults all had worry written on their foreheads, even as they tried to smile and make the best of it with the kids, many of whom were clustered around Minnie, petting her and laughing at her little pig noises.

"Emotional support pig," I said.

"She definitely is," Laura agreed.

We sat down in the secluded spot away from the chaos of

everyone else. It almost felt like hiding, but for now, I was okay with that.

"What are we going to tell them?" I said.

"We don't have to tell them anything. It's not like they can read minds."

I stared at her.

"Laura, have you seen my face? This is not a secret-keeping face." I pointed at myself.

"They don't need to even know there's a secret. Just act normally."

I didn't know how to do that. Probably good that we'd be out of the inn for most of the day.

"Listen, I can drive, if you want. My car is bigger."

Michelle came to take our drink orders and I could barely look at her, but I could feel her staring at me and then glancing at Laura and back. Laura kicked me lightly under the table.

I was trying. I was trying to be normal like I hadn't been having a naked pillow fight with her less than an hour before.

"I'll get those drinks for you," Michelle said in a weird voice. I didn't look up from the tablecloth until she left.

"She was being weird. That was weird, right? She probably knows," I hissed at Laura.

"You need to calm down," Laura said in a soothing voice. "You're freaking out about nothing. Even if she does suspect something, we're not going to say anything, so she won't know if it's just her imagination."

I had to admit that was a good point, but I was starting to crack under the stress of thinking that everyone knew that Laura and I hooked up.

"Good morning girls," Lillian said, and I smiled at her.

"Looks like Minnie is having a good time," I said. The pig was literally in the middle of a pile of giggling children.

"I'm glad she's helping take their mind off it. I heard you're going out to get a few things for them, and would you mind getting some ornaments? We're going to get an extra tree so they can all decorate it together tonight."

How sweet. Laura added that to our list and I had the feeling before we got back from shopping, that list was going to balloon and my car was going to be full.

Before we finished breakfast, there were more additions to Laura's list. I was tired from the night before, but I was going to suck it up. The breakfast restored me a little bit, and two cups of coffee helped even more.

"You ready to go?" I asked Laura, as we took our own dishes into the kitchen. It seemed like the right thing to do.

"Yeah," Laura said, giving me a look. It was the kind of look that said she wanted to drag me into the deep freezer and maybe do some things that might melt the ice in there.

"You can't look at me like that," I whispered, looking around, but there was no one around.

"I can't help it," she said. "I'll do my best, but no promises."

I groaned and she pushed me through the laundry room again and out the door.

~

SINCE THE INN was located in such a rural area, we had to drive quite a distance to find a big box store that would have everything we needed.

"Okay, let's do the clothes first," Laura said, looking at her list. I was going to let her take charge on this since she was the most organized of the two of us. I both loved and hated that aspect of her personality.

"We'll start with the kids and work our way up. Okay. There are two little girl toddlers."

I had literally never shopped for toddler clothes before, so it was a little bit of a learning curve, but we found pants, shirts, socks, underwear, and a few sweaters. They'd managed to escape with their coats, but we got extras just in case.

"I hope they like pink and purple because that's all there is here," Laura said.

"Can we grab some stuff in the same sizes from the boy's section just to make sure? Then whatever they don't want we can donate."

Laura liked that idea, so we did the same thing in the boy's section. We'd forgotten that they needed pajamas, so we added those as well, and then ticked off the rest of the people on the list.

Shoes were next, followed by basics like toothbrushes, and then some other random supplies they'd requested. Somehow we managed to fill one cart, so Laura sent me to the front of the store for a second.

That got filled with Christmas ornaments and tinsel and then we went bananas in the toy aisle.

"They all need stuffed animals, that's for sure," I said, throwing anything cute and fluffy into the cart.

"Okay, dolls and blocks, and some puzzles, and games, and I think we're good. Someone is going to donate electronics, so I hope they aren't disappointed that we didn't get tablets for them."

"Something tells me they aren't going to be disappointed," I said.

"Maybe not. I just want them to have a good Christmas, or at least a non-shitty one. I can't imagine losing everything."

I agreed, so we put some extra toys in the cart and then went to check out. I almost fainted at the bill, but Laura didn't bat an eyelash as she handed over the credit card.

We loaded up the car and headed back to the inn, but not before stopping to grab a fast food snack of fries and milk-shakes. The two of us sat in the parking lot, munching fries and sipping on cool sweetness and I couldn't remember the last time I'd done anything like this.

"I think we should wrap up the presents when we get back."

I agreed, even though I probably wouldn't do a very good job. It was the thought that counted, right?

"Hey," she said, turning in the passenger seat to face me.

"What?" I asked, putting my milkshake in the cup holder.

"Can I kiss you?"

"Yeah, you can kiss me."

The console was between us, so that was a little awkward, but we made it work. She kissed me and I kissed her back and my heart did that warm and fluttery thing and I never wanted it to end.

Laura's phone buzzed and she groaned.

"We have to get snacks for kids, apparently. There's a list."

Back to the store we went.

~

IT WAS dark when we finally got back.

"I'm so exhausted and I'm starving." Fortunately, it was time for dinner, but we still had to unload everything. We put all the presents in the barn and took everything else into the inn.

"Oh my goodness," Liana said, coming out to help us. "I think you went a little overboard, but there's no such thing as overboard in this situation, thank you."

The families were at dinner and Laina decided she didn't want to make a big thing of it, so we all snuck upstairs and left the items in each of the rooms they were staying in. It was almost like being Santa.

"Thank you so much for helping, I know it's going to make

a difference." Laina put one arm around me and one around Laura and hugged us both at the same time.

She let us go and I was a little embarrassed.

"We're starving so we're going back down to dinner," Laura said, speaking for both of us.

"Go ahead," Laina said and gave me a wink before I followed Laura down the stairs.

"I think your mom knows," I said to her, as we got to the bottom of the stairs.

"Probably. She doesn't miss much. Remind me to tell you about the one and only time I tried to sneak out and how it went."

I definitely wanted to hear that story, so I made a note to ask later.

We got swept into the arms of her family again and it was impossible to sit at our little table alone. No, we had to dine with everyone.

Laura was seated next to me and I spent the entirety of the dinner completely aware of her, and aware of everyone staring at me and wondering what had changed between Laura and me.

After only a few minutes, I was entirely convinced that everyone at the table knew exactly what had happened between me and Laura last night. They might not know the exact details (since they weren't mind readers), but they knew that *something* had happened, and things between us had changed.

I got sidetracked by a conversation with Dan and Lillian about Christmas traditions, but I heard Laura talking about me to Mel.

"Yeah, they're staying with me for now."

My heart skipped a beat hearing her using the right pronoun for me. I felt something on my leg and put my hand under the table to find her fingers there, as if she'd been waiting for me.

I squeezed her fingers and she took her hand back. I didn't think anyone had noticed, but I could barely breathe and had to remember what I'd been talking about.

Laura got up when she'd finished dinner and went to the piano. I followed her, of course.

"You know, you don't have to always be playing. You can just sit and be."

"I know," she said, playing a few quick scales. "But it saves me from having to answer probing questions from my nosy relatives."

Oh, good point.

I sat next to her on the bench again and she asked me for song suggestions and played every one.

"You're incredible," I said, and it was a battle not to kiss her. I'd never wanted to kiss anyone so much in my entire life.

"So are you," she said. "You have no idea."

I didn't think I was all that great, but I wasn't going to argue with her while she was playing. Instead, I sat and listened as she wove a web of music and comfort around me.

Abruptly, she stopped and turned to me.

"Why are we here when we could be in my room doing other things?" she asked.

I blinked at her for a second.

"I have absolutely no idea. Let's go."

It was hard not to run out of the inn and back to Laura's room. We at least had to say goodnight to people. After the long day and the little sleep I'd gotten the night before, I was exhausted, so it wasn't a total lie that Laura and I were going to bed early. It would be earlier than last night, I hoped.

"Wait," she said, as we stripped off our winter clothes in the foyer of her parent's house.

"What?" I kicked off my boots and I was ready to strip off my clothes too.

"We should bring snacks with us."

"I swear to god, if you spend an hour arranging another charcuterie tray, Laura," I said, as I hung up my coat.

"No, no, I won't do that. But we should have sustenance for in between." That was so Laura, planning snacks for our sexcapades.

She grabbed some crackers, cheese, fruit, waters, and a few other odds and ends and loaded up her arms before we went upstairs to her room. She dumped all the snacks on the dresser and turned to face me.

"Now," she said. "Where were we?"

I laughed.

"That was such a movie line, Laura. Why don't you ask me what color my underwear is?"

She took a seductive step toward me.

"What color are your panties, Colden?"

I pulled the waist of my jeans out and looked.

"Uh, they're kind of white with polka dots, and lace on the edges."

"Really?" She dropped the sexy act and came over. "They sound cute."

"What color are yours?"

"Do you want to see?"

"Obviously," I said, rolling my eyes. "I mean, if we're being honest, I kind of don't care, but I was playing along with the sexy talk. Sorry, I'm not good at this." I was killing the mood.

"Come here," she said, hooking her fingers around my belt loops and pulling me so I crashed into her. "You're doing really well as far as I'm concerned."

This was the first time we'd kissed standing up and it was a whole new experience. Our height difference of about six inches made things interesting. Being the shorter one, I pushed up on my tiptoes to reach her and she leaned down and we met in the middle, trying to learn how to angle our faces so we didn't bump noses and so both of us could breathe. Kissing required a lot of maneuvering when you were standing up.

"Come on," she said, walking backwards, pulling me with her. "Let's do a little prep before we get into this."

I stared at her. What kind of prep was she talking about? Then she opened the drawer in her nightstand and pulling out a few things.

"Can you grab a towel from the closet in my bathroom? One of the bigger ones." I didn't blame her for not wanting to have to wash the sheets for the second day in a row.

When I got back with the towel, she had quite the array of . . . things.

"So, you can have your pick of lube. I recommend this one," she said, pointing to a bottle. There were also several toys laid out. That was a relief. I had been hoping she'd be open to using them, or at least familiar with them and wouldn't think I was a weirdo for having one.

I dove for my suitcase and pulled out my trusty friend who had delighted me for many hours.

Laura held up the same toy in a different color.

"Twins," she said.

I walked back toward the bed and saw what else she had.

"What's this?" I asked, pointing to what looked like a harness.

Laura took a deep breath before she answered. "It's a strap on. Goes with either of these."

"Oh," I said. I'd never used one, but had always wondered.

"It's brand new, I haven't used it. In case you were worried about that. It was kind of a joke, but then I kept it and, well, I wouldn't be upset if it was used."

"By me or on me?" I asked.

She lifted one shoulder "Either. Both."

"Oh," I said again. I'd thought we were going to do the same shit as last night, but Laura had brought out so many accessories that my mind reeled with the possibilities.

"We don't have to do anything tonight. I just wanted to show you that there were options and I'm open to a lot of things. Maybe I should have waited, but I was too excited."

I looked at her and there was a shy smile on her face. She'd been excited to show me her sex toys. How adorable.

"Thank you for sharing this with me," I said, kissing her. "I don't know if we'll get through everything tonight, because that seems like a lot of batteries, but I'm definitely up for adding a little something, if you want." I knew I wanted. I always had the most powerful orgasms when I had a little help from my buzzing friend. If Laura was using it on me? Mind-blowing.

"Let's get naked," she said, slapping my butt.

"Ooohhhh, do that again," I said leaning over.

"Really? Okay." She spanked me again and I shivered in pleasure.

"Yes, more of that later, definitely."

～

ROUND ONE WAS JUST lips and tongues and fingers and grinding and lube. This time she let me go first and she went second. We both decided a break was in order before we did anything else.

"What are you thinking about?" I asked as we twisted and untwisted our fingers together. We'd left the lights on this time, and it was a whole lot easier to see what I was doing.

"I'm thinking that maybe I'd like to try fucking you," I said. The thought had taken root and bloomed in my mind and I couldn't get it out of my head until I'd at least tried it.

"Yeah?" she said, sitting up.

"Yeah."

What followed was me hilariously trying to get the freaking harness on and fitting right before picking which dildo she wanted to use.

"This is interesting."

"Do you ever wish you had a dick?" she asked.

"Not really. I'm pretty happy with what I have, but it's fun to think about." I stared down at my new appendage as Laura lubed it up.

The harness wasn't the most comfortable thing, but I didn't plan on wearing it for long.

"I'm not going to lie, that looks so fucking hot," Laura said, stroking the dildo.

She looked hot, doing that.

"You ready?" I asked.

Laura nodded and lay back on the bed. I climbed up and positioned myself in the right spot, but I wanted to kiss her a bit before I went for it, so I did.

She opened up to me and I moved the dildo so it teased her entrance and she moaned.

"Quiet," I said. "You have to be quiet, baby." I hadn't called her that outside of the bedroom, thankfully. That would have been a very obvious clue that something had gone on between us.

"I'm trying," she said, and then I slowly pushed inside her and she jacked off the bed and let out a loud moan.

"Oh, fuck that feels so good, Colden." I loved hearing her say my name, but hearing her saying it during sex was a whole other level.

I pulled my hips back a little too far and the dildo fell out, so there was a learning curve to using it, but once I got the hang of it? I fucked her so hard she came twice in succession and I almost came myself just from the rush of power.

I held onto her as the second climax passed through her and hushed her sounds as best I could.

"We are definitely doing this again," I said in her ear, before I rolled off and onto my back. The harness had rubbed in certain areas, so I made a mental note to search for one online that would fit better and not chafe.

"Are we?" she said, turning on her side and stroking my belly.

"Definitely. That was awesome."

Laura started fiddling with the harness and before I knew what was happening, she'd gotten it undone and off me and was poised above me, holding my vibrator.

"Fuck, this is the best thing that's ever happened to me," I said.

"You made me come twice, so that means I get to make you come three times. It's only fair." I wanted to argue, but she turned the vibrator on and I forgot how to speak.

Laura wielded the vibrator like she played the piano. She played my body with it, going hard and then soft, moving it from this area to another, torturing me until I was almost screaming and the only thing that stopped me was the house full of people who would hear me. This was a time when a remote cottage by the ocean would have been useful.

Laura drove me to the first of three earth-shattering, mind-bending, body-destroying orgasms, and I didn't know if I could move afterward. My entire body felt as if I'd had my bones removed, or at least replaced with rubber.

The room was quiet as she turned the vibrator off and set it aside.

"That was fun. I'd go again, but I don't know if you could take it." She kissed me and we lay together and basked in the post-coital glow.

I ran my fingers through her hair and she yawned and I asked her if she was hungry.

"Yeah, a little bit. See, it was smart to bring the snacks in." I got up and stumbled a little before I made it over to the dresser and filled my arms with the snacks and tossed them on the bed next to all the vibrators.

"I think we can put those away for now, but I want to clean them first," Laura said. She got up and put them all in the bathroom as I lay out a few of the snacks and opened a water for her.

"Cracker?" I said, holding one up.

She opened her mouth and I fed her. I was surprised she wasn't worried about crumbs on the bed, but she didn't say anything as she munched and chewed. I held up a piece of cheese and she opened her mouth again. Laura and I fed each other until we were sated and I looked at the clock.

"I want to fuck you again, but I might fall asleep, and that would be too embarrassing. Do you want to take a quick shower and go to sleep?"

She agreed and we cleaned up the snacks, washed the vibrators, and showered. So orderly, so clean.

I climbed into Laura's bed for the second night and she held me. We were both naked again, which I wasn't used to, but being naked with Laura was better than not being naked with Laura.

She settled against me and there were those pesky thoughts again. The ones I'd managed to outrun by being so busy and distracted today.

What the hell was I doing with Laura? What was I doing here at this inn and hanging out with her family? What was I doing here?

Those thoughts weren't pleasant, and they didn't give me good feelings at all. I tried to push them aside, but I couldn't. The thoughts persisted, telling me that I needed to leave, I needed to get out of here before I got my heart broken yet again.

In addition to my mom leaving, and my dad dying, I'd also had my best friend and every person I'd ever dated break up with me. Not a nice feeling. When so many people in your life left you, it made you think that you were the problem. That you were unlovable. That no one wanted you.

Laura seemed to want me, but I wasn't sure. I didn't understand it. Surely she'd come to her senses eventually and realize that she could have anyone she wanted, and that whatever we had was a one-time thing.

Were Christmas flings a thing? Getting so caught up in the holiday spirit that you banged someone you wouldn't normally bang? I suppose anything was possible.

Eventually, my exhausted body shut my mind down long enough for sleep, but when I awoke, the thoughts and doubts and insecurities were still going to be there. Fucking Laura yet again wasn't going to change them, but that's what I did before I did anything else that morning.

"Sorry, I couldn't help myself. You just looked so delectable," I said, coming up for air and wiping my face. I needed another shower.

"You're a mess," she laughed.

"I'm a sloppy eater." That made her laugh even harder and then I went to wash my face and get dressed for the day. Laura had to serve at lunch and dinner tonight, but we would have breakfast together.

"Merry Christmas Eve Eve," she said, kissing me as I looked in the mirror and tried to decide if my outfit was going to work or not.

"Merry Christmas Eve Eve," I said back. My dysphoria was quiet today, which was a blessing. A Christmas miracle.

"Come on, I'm starving."

She held my hand and I had to break the contact before we left the room again.

"I don't like that. I want to hold your hand."

"That's a song," I said.

"Colden. Are we ever going to talk about this?"

I didn't want to, but I'd have to. This wasn't going to go away when Christmas was over. We'd be back in Boston and back at work, and that was going to be awkward as fuck if we didn't sort it out now.

"Later," I said. I still needed to get my thoughts in order, and even figure out what my thoughts were. Right now it was a jumble of chaos and lust in my brain. Not exactly coherent.

"Okay. But I'm not putting this off. You're going to have to talk to me and you can't distract me with sex forever."

It was as if she'd read my thoughts.

"Come on, let's go eat." She opened the door and led the way back to the inn.

Chapter Ten

"Mistletoe!" someone yelled, and I flinched. I'd been avoiding that shit since I got here and I'd gotten distracted by Laura and hadn't noticed the new cluster hung at the entrance to the dining room.

Where I was currently standing with Laura.

"Come on, it's mistletoe," Lillian said, and just about everyone turned to see what was happening.

"Oh my god, I want to die," I whispered.

"It's fine. We'll just do it and that will shut them up," Laura said. "Ready?"

Before I could answer, she spun me to face her and planted her lips on me. After a moment of shock, I kissed her back like a reflex and then I heard hoots and cheers and had to forcibly separate myself from Laura's mouth.

Her cheeks were flushed and her eyes sparkled as she smiled at me.

"Oops," she said.

I closed my eyes and took a breath before I turned to face everyone in the dining room who'd been watching. There were knowing smiles on nearly every face, and curiosity on others who didn't know who Laura and I were.

"K-I-S-S-I-N-G," a child sang, and was quickly hushed by a parent.

"Should we say anything?" I whispered to Laura, as they continued to stare.

"No, leave them in suspense." She swept by me and headed for our usual out-of-the-way table.

I could feel everyone glancing over and whispering and talking about us. It was pretty disconcerting.

"Will you calm down? People kiss under mistletoe all the time. See?" Antonio had come out from the kitchen and he and Laina shared a quick but sweet kiss to cheers and hoots. I rarely saw the two interacting, so it was almost strange to see them sharing a moment like that together.

"Your parents are married," I pointed out. "It's pretty normal for them to be kissing."

One good thing was that Michelle didn't come to take our orders. It was another cousin of Laura's who seemed a little frazzled and was too concerned with getting all the orders right to be thinking about me and Laura sharing a kiss.

I kept my attention on my plate, but I couldn't stop the feeling that everyone was watching the two of us as if we were the most interesting reality show they'd ever seen.

"We're a spectacle," I whispered to Laura, as I added ketchup to my plate for the potatoes.

"Don't worry, one of my aunts will do something and everyone will forget about it."

I wasn't so sure.

"It's already done, Colden. We can't really unkiss."

No, we couldn't. I was just going to do my best to act normally in this abnormal situation.

Merry Christmas Eve Eve to me.

SINCE LAURA HAD to work most of the day, I told Laina I'd get a head start on wrapping the presents for the families. I'd met all of them by now and the kids were so darn cute and always running around and chasing Minnie, so it added an extra layer of noise and chaos, but I wasn't upset about it. Something must be happening to me because usually a bunch of kids running around and screaming would make me run and hide, or at least beg for a book and some noise-cancelling headphones.

The holiday cheer was infecting my brain.

I wasn't much of a present wrapper, but I did my best and got a bunch of the toys done before drifting back over to the inn to see what was going on. I'd spent less than an hour alone today and I was ready to go back and be surrounded by people again.

Who was I becoming?

CHRISTMAS ACTIVITIES WERE in full force when I got back, with the kids taking over the dining room for finger painting. Laina looked like she was trying to enjoy herself, but was also worried about the wallpaper and the carpets.

Laura handed out cups of water and Michelle sat with one little girl and helped her dip her hands in the paint.

I expected Laina to say something about the kiss with her daughter, but she didn't.

"There's plenty of supplies, if you want to get on in there."

I shook my head.

"No, I think I'm good. Do you need any napkins or towels folded?"

"Sure, if you want. Or you could enjoy the time off and go hang out in the library."

That was what I wanted to do, but I also had the need to contribute, so I did both. I went to the laundry room and folded everything that needed to be folded and then carried it upstairs to the linen closets.

That task done, I went back to the library and picked up a book.

"Hey," a voice said, after I'd been reading for a few pages.

I looked up to see Laura standing there and smiling down at me.

"Do you wanna go sledding?"

I blinked at her for a few seconds.

"Sledding?"

"Yeah, we're taking a bunch of the kids sledding. We've got a bunch of old ones in the barn and it will get them out of their parent's hair for a little while. You in?"

"Uh, sure?"

"You don't sound sure."

I looked back at my book and then closed it.

"I'm sure," I said, standing up. I honestly couldn't remember the last time I'd gone sledding. It had probably been when I was a child, probably with my dad.

It took nearly an hour to get the kids suited up and ready to go out and make sure everyone had hats and mittens and had peed before they put on their snow pants.

Laura and I hauled the sleds while the kids tromped happily through the snow.

The property of the inn reached back into the woods, but there was an old path along a stone wall that led us to the back edge of a golf course mounted on a hill.

"Why would you put a golf course on a hill? Doesn't that defeat the purpose of golf?" I asked, but Laura just dragged me along with the sleds to the top of the golf-course hill where there were already a bunch of people sledding and laughing and having a great time.

"Okay," Laura announced to the kids. "Everyone gets a sled. Don't go into the trees. If you get hurt, scream so we hear you. Be safe. I don't want to take you back to your parents broken, okay?"

"Okay!" A bunch of little voices chimed in.

"Go!" Laura yelled and the kids squealed and lined up to take the long ride down the hill, screaming as they went.

"You want to ride?" Laura said, holding up a sled that would fit two of us. I was a little wary of the hill and the edges of trees on either side of the course, but everyone else seemed to be having a good time. I wasn't a *total* grump.

"As long as I get to steer," I said.

Laura held the sled steady as I got in and then she climbed in behind me, her legs on either side of me.

"You ready, Colden?" her warm voice said in my ear.

"As I'll ever be," I said, and then Laura used her arms to push us to the top of the hill and then we were flying.

I let out a scream as the sled hurtled down the hill and Laura screamed behind me, her hands gripping my arms so she didn't fall out of the sled.

At last we slowed down and, before the sled stopped, we ended up tipping over and spilling out onto the snow, both gasping with laughter.

I rolled over onto my back so I could breath and she lay next to me.

"That was fun."

"Yeah, let's do it again."

Laura sat up and turned the sled back over.

"The only bad part is we have to go back to the top." She pointed and I saw how far we'd come down the hill.

"Where's a ski lift when you need one?" I groaned, getting to my feet.

"Or a team of sled dogs," she added. "Come on." She held out her gloved hand to mine and I took it, hoping not one else was paying attention to the two people holding hands as they dragged their sled back up the hill.

I collapsed when we got to the top, completely winded.

"You ready for another run?" Laura asked, not winded at all.

"Give me a minute," I gasped, holding up my hand.

Once I'd recovered enough to get back in the sled, I positioned myself and this time Laura put her arms around my waist and her chin on my shoulder.

"Let's go, babe," she said, and the shock of the endearment hit me a second before someone gave us a push and we barreled down the hill again.

∼

I LOST count of how many runs we made, but we had to gather up the kids because Laura had to get back for the lunch shift. They were all red-cheeked and giddy, talking about coming again and hot chocolate and whose sled was the fastest.

I was completely worn out when we got back to the inn, but the kids seemed to have boundless energy. Michelle was waiting with a pot full of hot cocoa as the stripped off their coats and snow pants and mittens and hats.

"Can we bottle some of that and use it for ourselves?" I asked, as they bounced and cheered and chattered and raced for the cocoa.

"I wish," Laura said. "Listen, I'll see you later? I have to go memorize the specials." She gave me a big fake smile and then headed back to the kitchen.

I was messing on my phone when I looked up and saw Michelle.

"Hey," she said, in a too-loud voice.

"Hey," I said, cringing internally. I had a feeling I knew what was coming, and I wanted to run away. I wished I had a good excuse.

"Can I talk to you for a second?" she asked.

Pretending I had no idea what this could possibly be about, I said, "sure."

I followed Michelle into a corner of the empty library.

"So, uh, what was with you and Laura under the mistletoe this morning? It looked pretty . . . yeah." She hadn't been able to come up with a word.

"Honestly, I'm not really sure. But there might be something? Please don't say anything to anyone." I didn't know if I could trust Michelle with this information. If this got to one member of the Sterling family, my feeling was that it would get to all of them.

"Oh, yeah, sure. No problem." Her voice squeaked and I could tell she was crestfallen.

"It just kind of happened. We didn't plan anything. She's been pissing me off at work for a year and now . . . I have no idea." I laughed, but it wasn't really funny.

"Yeah, shit happens," Michelle said, looking at the floor. "Um, I should get back to work."

"You should go," I said, just as she was about to leave the room.

"Huh?"

"You should go to Boston and stay with Laura. See what the city is all about. Figure out who you want to be, outside of this," I waved around to the inn. "Or don't, but know that the option is there and it's yours."

She nodded and bit her lip before walking away without saying anything else.

I guess that went as well as it could have gone. I really hoped she came to Boston, even if it would be awkward for a while. She'd see that there were tons of people she could date that weren't me. The only reason she'd latched on was that I was new and shiny and not related to her.

∽

IN BETWEEN LUNCH AND DINNER, Laura and I took a slow walk. My legs were still jelly from the sledding earlier, but it had just started to snow, and Laura wanted to take some pictures, so I agreed to go with her.

Laura took some pictures on her phone of the inn and the lights on the porch before asking me to pose.

"No, I'm good," I said. Pictures sometimes made me feel weird.

"Are you sure? You look great right now with the snow on your eyelashes."

"I guess," I said. "But I get veto power on any images and you have to delete them."

Laura held her phone up and angled the shot.

"Deal."

I didn't know if I was supposed to pose or not so I just kind of stood there.

"Okay, turn a little to the left? The light is perfect." I posed and she gave me directions and then we started walking and she kept randomly snapping pics of me.

"I very much doubt any of these is good," I said. I wasn't a huge fan of pictures of myself.

"No, they're good. Want to see?"

Not really, but she handed me the phone and I scrolled through the pictures. They weren't horrible. Instead of taking all of them of my whole face, she'd focused on my features. My eyes, my profile, my lips. She'd taken a few while I was talking and smiling without realizing it.

I looked amazing. I didn't know how she'd done it, but she'd captured . . . me. Me, distilled down to my essence.

"Wow," I said. There were a few that I didn't like, so I deleted those, but the majority were good.

"Can you send me those?" I asked.

"Absolutely. You really do look amazing."

She put her phone in her pocket and grabbed my jacket, using it to bring me closer.

"Can I kiss you in the snow?"

"Yeah, you can kiss me in the snow."

Laura kissed me in the snow, and the snow melted on my eyelashes.

∼

WE WALKED BACK in the woods, near the path we'd taken the kids on to get to the golf course.

"It's so quiet out here." Every now and then you'd hear the distant sound of a car. Otherwise, snow fell from the trees as they creaked in the breeze.

"Yeah, this is something I do miss. The serenity. Hard to get in the city when you're always surrounded by people."

It was true, you couldn't get a whole lot of privacy or alone time in Boston. That was one of the reasons why I'd wanted to come to Maine in the first place. For the solitude.

Funnily enough, I was enjoying my solitude with Laura. It was nearly as good as being alone.

Laura hummed a tune under her breath and took my hand.

"I think we're safe here."

That reminded me of the conversation I'd had with Michelle and I told Laura about it.

"She'll keep her mouth shut. When I came out to her, she came out to me at the same time and we kept each other's secret until we could tell our parents. She's solid."

That made me feel a little bit better, but I was still a little worried about everyone making up their own mind what Laura and I were doing.

"Speaking of that, what are we doing, Colden? Are you ready to talk about it?"

I wasn't, but we had to.

"I don't know, Laura, I honestly don't. This is still so new and I'm confused and can we just . . . ride it out through Christmas and regroup when we get back to Boston? It's too hard to think right now." Too much holiday spirit clouding my judgment.

"That's fair. So you're still okay with doing what we're doing until we get back to Boston?"

I was more than okay with it, actually.

"Absolutely. I want to see you wear that strap on, baby," I said, and she burst out laughing.

"I don't think I'm going to look as hot as you wearing it, but I'll give it a shot."

We argued about who was hotter until our noses got too cold to continue staying outside and we headed back to the inn.

Laura snuck a kiss on the porch before we walked inside and I knew we were being reckless, but I didn't care. It was Christmas Eve Eve.

Chapter Eleven

Dinner that night was festive and noisy. The Sterlings had absorbed the extra people already and things were going well. The kids seemed happy and the adults were doing their best, between taking calls about insurance and dealing with the fire inspector.

Donations had also been flooding in, and Laina had to section off part of the library for all the gifts and supplies people kept dropping off. I couldn't lie, it made me pretty emotional to see how this town took care of its own.

I couldn't get enough of being with Laura. Whenever she was gone, I was always glancing over my shoulder to see if she was going to come around the corner. I kept thinking of things I wanted to say to her.

I only had a few more days here, and I didn't know what it was going to be like to leave here and go back to normal. Granted, I didn't have to think about things like making dinner or cleaning my apartment when I was here, but still. Being with the Sterlings was like being wrapped in the warmest, most wonderful weighted blanket. They made me feel wanted.

The activity of the night was apparently the kids putting on a play they'd written and practiced all afternoon which was a mashup of *The Grinch*, *Charlie Brown*, and some popular kid's TV show I'd never heard of. They had costumes and a set and props and everything. It was painfully cute and they got a standing ovation from everyone in the dining room.

Afterwards, they were rewarded with more cookies than they could possibly eat and more hot chocolate. The adults partook in mulled wine and eggnog, and I sat with Laura while we watched the little ones mess around on the piano.

"Aren't you worried they're going to break something?" I asked, as little hands slapped down on the keys, making dissonant sounds.

"No, that piano is pretty tough. I think it can take it." She sipped from her mug of mulled wine and studied me.

"What are you thinking about?" I asked.

"What do you think?" she asked, raising one eyebrow.

"Oh, I'm guessing it's not anything that you can talk about in public."

She pointed at me. "Bingo." I think she was starting to get a little tipsy, and I was curious to see how she'd be if she'd had a few.

"I'm eager to see what you have in mind."

"I'll bet you are." She smiled at me and then started giggling.

"You're so cute right now."

"You're cute right now." She leaned over the table and motioned for me to come closer. "I wish I could kiss you right now."

I wanted that too. For a second, I allowed myself to think about what that would be like, if I let her kiss me in front of everyone and then we could just . . . be together.

If only we could do that without questions from everyone. They would want to know everything, when it started, what we were going to do when we got back to Boston, if we were serious. I didn't think either of us was ready for any of that. All of this was happening so fucking fast and I was along for the ride. At least we could try and control who knew what and when.

"Soon you can kiss me," I whispered back.

"Not soon enough."

She sat back and pouted before finishing her cup of wine.

The evening started to wind down and Laura had some more wine, and I wanted to laugh at how silly she got. She wasn't drunk by any means, but she was definitely getting there.

"Come on, baby," I said softly to her. "Let's go to bed."

Her eyes lit up.

"Hell yeah, let's do that."

I shushed her, but she just laughed and I knew that it was time for us to head to her room.

"Come here," she said, the second the door to her room closed, giving me a sloppy kiss.

"Hey, slow down," I said, putting my hand on her chest to put some space between us.

"Let's have some snacks first, okay?"

She pouted again, but sat on the bed.

I fed her again and she started yawning. I didn't think anything sexy was going to happen tonight, which was fine. Instead I pushed her into the shower and joined her, soaping up her body while she tried to stay awake.

"Note to self, wine makes Laura sleepy."

"Not always. But tonight for some reason." She yawned again and leaned on me as I scrubbed her back.

I got her into pajamas and under the covers where she snuggled up into a ball like an adorable little creature.

"You're so cute right now, I can barely stand it," I said, as I put on my own pajamas and then got in next to her.

"Come here, baby," I said, and she scooted over so I could

wrap her in my arms. She was so warm and I breathed in the scent of her freshly-washed hair.

"I'm not going to let myself fall in love with you," I whispered so low that she couldn't hear it. "I won't let it happen."

She mumbled something in a sleepy voice.

"Go to sleep, Laura."

She mumbled something else and then I heard a soft snoring noise. She was out.

~

THE NEXT MORNING I woke to find her watching me.

"Weirdo," I said.

"I've only been watching you sleep for a few hours," she said in a creepy voice, making her eyes wide.

"Okay, now I'm scared. This has been your whole game, hasn't it? The long con."

She shook her head.

"No, I have no idea what you're talking about, Colden. I would never ingratiate myself into your life and then slowly take on your identity and then poison you and stuff your body in a deep freezer. I'm not that kind of girl."

My eyes narrowed.

"That was all extremely specific."

"Hey, you ready for breakfast?" She bounded out of bed and spun around to face me, her hair flying everywhere.

"You're trying to change the subject, and it scares me." I stretched out and looked at the clock. I hadn't slept in as much as I'd like on this vacation. I was still on work time.

"I'm *so* hungry, aren't you?" she said in a singsong voice.

"You are deliberately evading my questions, Laura." I got up and went through my suitcase of clothes. My options were dwindling as far as what I had to wear. I'd need to do laundry before I went home.

"I wish we could spend all day in bed," Laura said, hugging me from behind, kissing my cheek.

"I mean, we could, but then people would have questions. We could both say we're sick, but I have the feeling there would be too many people trying to nurse us and that would defeat the purpose."

Laura sighed and then kissed my other cheek before letting me go.

"I mean, we don't have to stop once we get back to Boston. We can just . . . keep going."

That wasn't the deal.

"We'll figure that out when we get back. Can't we just enjoy the time we have now and not worry about the future?" I was so sick of thinking about the future and watching it stretch bleakly out in front of me.

True, I'd thought my lot in life was being alone and I'd mostly accepted that. My plan had been to get a bunch of dogs and do a lot of volunteering.

"Yeah, we can. Sorry, I won't bug you about it again."

I stripped off my pajamas and started to put my clothes on.

"Mmmm, that's what I'm talking about," she said, and I turned around. I'd been pulling my undies on.

"Are you ogling me?" I asked, pretending to be scandalized.

"Yes, I am."

I laughed and wiggled my ass for her.

"Yeah, back that thing up."

I danced back toward her and she grabbed my ass with both hands and pretended to spank it.

"We're such dorks," I said, standing up.

"At least we're both dorks. It would be hard to be the only dork in the relationship."

True.

I got dressed the rest of the way and we headed to breakfast.

"Mistletoe!" someone called out the second we walked under the arch. It was like they'd planned it.

Every face was waiting, expectantly.

"Again?" I asked Laura.

"Why not?"

We kissed again and I got weak at the knees and had to gather myself before I could walk to our table.

"We're not doing a good job of hiding this thing, Laura. I mean, we might as well come out and say that we're doing *something* together." If only I knew what that something was.

"We could. If you're up for it. There will be questions, but I can beg them to knock it off. I don't think it'll be as bad as you're assuming."

I mean, they were her family, so she probably knew better, but I still wasn't sure.

"We'll see. Let me eat something first."

I didn't have any more clarity after breakfast, but it was time for lots of Christmas festivities. Movies all day, tons of cookies, Laura played the piano until I begged her to rest her hands, we took the kids sledding again, and I ended up having to take a nap before dinner. Laura joined me and we had a cuddlefest that was just what I'd needed.

When we woke up, I rolled over and gave her a kiss. It could be like this all the time, if I wanted. I could stay at her (probably lavish) apartment and she'd make charcuterie trays and we could make out all the time.

But what would happen at work? It would be weird to shift that kind of relationship to the workday. It would be too weird, wouldn't it?

How could we interact professionally if we were fucking at night? I mean, I knew it could be done, but did I really want to?

Too many questions, not enough answers.

"You're thinking awfully hard over there, babe," she said, pressing her finger between my eyebrows.

"Sorry, can't help it." I kissed her so I'd forget, and it worked for a little while. Then it was back to hang out with the rest of the Sterlings and more food and more warm drinks and more movies and holiday cheer.

I'd done more Christmas in the past two weeks than I'd ever done in my life, not even with my dad. Sure, he'd loved Christmas, but we hadn't made a whole marathon out of it. Some cookies, *The Grinch*, a list to Santa, and that had been it. I didn't even remember having a wreath on the door, ever.

I still had some of the family ornaments in my storage facility. I'd almost forgotten about them. I'd boxed so many things away that I had forgotten about.

The kids were amped up and pretty much running wild when dinner came around, so Laina got them set up in the library with beanbags and another movie with lobster mac and cheese. The adults just had regular lobster.

"I think I've only had lobster like twice in my life," I said, looking at the red thing on my plate. It definitely looked like a bug, but from what I remembered, it was delicious.

"Here we go," Laura said, tying a plastic bib around my neck and then handing me a metal object.

"This is a lobster cracker."

Laura demonstrated how to use the cracker on the shell and extract the meat inside, dip it in clarified butter, and then enjoy.

"Oh, that is good," I said after my first bite.

I stuffed myself with lobster and clams and corn and salad and wine and then the gingerbread cake for dessert.

"I couldn't eat another thing," I said, sitting back and putting my hands on my stomach. It was a good thing these jeans were a little loose.

"That was so good," I said, and turned to thank Antonio.

"You're very welcome, Colden. It's nice to have someone who appreciates my food."

Laura rolled her eyes.

Raucous children's laugher kept booming from the library. I had no idea what they were watching, but it sounded like they were having fun.

"It's almost time for *White Christmas*," Laura said. "How about if you and I skip it and you can help me do some things back at the house?"

I caught her meaning immediately and we escaped to back to the house. I realized that my present for Laura had been delivered, so I grabbed it.

"What's that?"

"Just ordered something for myself. Figured it was easier to get it shipped here."

She still seemed suspicious, so I hurried her next door and shoved her up the stairs so I could distract her from thinking about what was in the box with sex. At least I tried to.

After kissing for a few moments, she pulled back.

"Did you get me a Christmas present?"

"What? No." Damn my truth-telling face.

"You totally did! What did you get me?"

I sighed. So much for the surprise.

"I'm not going to tell you because you don't get it until tomorrow. That's how Christmas works. If you don't like it, take it up with Santa."

She rested her hands on my shoulders.

"Okay, fine. But I got you something, so we'll be even tomorrow."

"You got me something?" That filled me with more joy than I wanted to admit.

"Yeah, I had to get you something. Actually, I've been holding onto it for a while." Her cheeks went red.

"Really?"

"I've been saving it for the right moment. This Christmas kind of feels right."

It did, in more ways than one.

I didn't know what to say, so I kissed her and then we removed each other's clothes and fucked slowly, softly. We'd have to go back after the movie, but there was a lot we could do in two hours.

She rode my face and then I rode her hand and we finished off with one vibrator between the two of us.

"I don't want to jinx it, but we're like, really good at sex," she said, as we recovered.

"Yeah, we are. That probably means we should keep doing it. You know, we owe it to sex."

She nodded and propped herself on her elbows.

"You're absolutely right. It would be a crime for us not to fuck as much as we could."

"I'm so glad we're on the same page about this."

We got dressed again and Laura helped me tame my hair into some sort of order before we walked together back to the inn. The movie was just wrapping up and it was time for the pajamas.

"Oh god, I'd forgotten about this," I said, when Laina handed me a package with a wink.

"You're an honorary Sterling, so here you go."

I looked down at the present and then at Laura.

"If you can't beat them, join them," she said.

Everyone got together and opened their presents, finding long pants and tops with red and green plaid and penguins on them. Too cute.

"Okay, everyone, go put on your pajamas, and then it's time for the fashion show," Laina said, clapping her hands together.

Laura dragged me to the public bathroom on the first floor and we changed together.

"You look so fucking cute right now, I can barely deal," she said, making me do a twirl.

"So do you. Who knew plaid was your color?"

She kissed me before we rejoined the rest of the family. A sea of plaid greeted us, along with an actual piece of red carpet, and some music that was supposed to sound like it was from a fashion show.

They'd even dressed Minnie up in a child-sized shirt and a bow on top of her head.

"Everyone line up," Liana said, still elegant even in the silly pajamas.

We all lined up and, one-by-one, headed down the catwalk. A few people danced or had moves, but some did the classic model walk, complete with sexy mad face.

Within a few minutes I was laughing so hard I could barely stand up, and when it was my turn, I decided to do a little dance to the music, complete with booty shaking and twirls.

When it was Laura's turn, she did a perfect model walk, and her hair even blew like she had a wind machine on her. She did several poses at the end and then purposely turned to me in the audience, and blew me a kiss.

Out of reflex, I caught it and pretended to put it in my pocket.

My second-favorite walk was Lillian, who strutted her stuff with Minnie at her side to cheers from everyone.

We were all given scorecards and I ranked Lillian the highest, and Laura the second. Laina collected the cards and tallied the results.

"For the fifth year in a row, the winner is Lillian!" Lillian pretended to be shocked and fake-sobbed as she took her trophy.

"I couldn't have done this without all of you," she said, pointing to everyone. "Thank you."

There was another round of cheers and then the kids were

hustled off to bed where they probably wouldn't sleep. Laura and I hung around with everyone for a little while, and I was shocked not to have any questions about Laura. Nope, everything was about Christmas and traditions and favorite movies and arguing about Christmas carols.

Weird.

Laura and I headed back to the house and read in bed for a long time.

"This is the way to do Christmas, in my opinion," I said.

"Just wait until breakfast tomorrow. You thought dinner was bad, but breakfast is on a whole other level."

I couldn't wait.

"I can't believe I'm spending Christmas with you. I wanted to spend it alone."

"Did you really, though?" she asked.

"I mean, I thought I did. But now I don't know if I would have regretted it? I like being alone, but I think I also like being with people. I like being with your family."

That was a lie. I *loved* being with her family.

"You know I come up and visit once a month. You could come with me sometime. They'd all love to see you."

That was an idea I really was going to consider.

"And you can talk to me too. About your dad and everything."

I needed someone to talk to. I'd been getting by on my own for so long and it was too much. You needed people to confide in, to listen to you.

If nothing else, this experience had opened my eyes that I needed to reach out to people more and start trusting again. My heart was permanently broken, but that didn't mean I had to shut everyone out to try and protect myself. That just meant I was still hurting, but I was going it alone.

"No matter what happens with us, I want you to know that

I'm always here for you, okay? I'm here to talk to, to help you move, to keep you company, any of it or all of it."

She hugged me and I felt my heart beating hard and fast.

"Same," I said. "Same to you. If you need another person in your life, I'm happy to be there."

"I *definitely* need a Colden in my life."

~

I WOKE up earlier than I normally would have, and the first thing I did was glance out the window.

Snow. The temperature had been so warm the other day that everything on the ground had melted, so I hadn't thought it was going to happen. An actual, real, white Christmas. As if it had been planned that way.

Laura was still asleep and I took that opportunity to get her present. I hadn't had a chance to wrap it, but I hoped she wouldn't mind. I put the box on the edge of the bed and waited for her to wake up. It didn't take long.

"Merry Christmas, Laura," I said, kissing her.

"Merry Christmas, Colden."

"Do you want your present now? It's not wrapped, sorry."

"Can you hold on a few seconds so I can get yours?"

I agreed and she made me close my eyes and promise not to peek.

She came back with a little package that had a bow on it.

"See, now I look like an asshole because I didn't wrap yours." I sighed.

"Will letting you open yours first make up for it?"

I took the present from her.

"I guess that's okay." I tore open the wrapping and found a long necklace with two silver discs on it. One was engraved SHE and the other was engraved THEY.

"Do you hate it?" she asked, when I didn't respond for a few seconds.

"No, I don't hate it," I said, trying to swallow my tears. It was so simple, but so pretty and so me. It was perfect.

I met her eyes and let myself cry.

"It's perfect, I love it."

Laura helped me put the necklace on and I looked down at it. I never wanted to take it off.

"Okay, yours isn't quite as good. But I hope you like it." Now I wish I'd spent more time on her gift. I was going to make up for it when we got back to Boston. I'd get her the perfect gift and give it to her as a late Christmas present.

"I'm sure I'll love it," she said.

She had to get up and grab a pair of scissors to get through the tape on the box.

"Oh, it's beautiful," she said, bringing out the wooden tray that would fit on the edge of her bathtub and had a platform to put her books on so she could read and soak at the same time. It also had places to put drinks and snacks.

"Are you sure? You're not just pretending you like it?" I wouldn't really know the difference.

"No, I actually do love it. It's perfect. I've wanted something like this for ages, but never would have bought it for myself. Thank you, Colden."

She kissed me and we got a little distracted with hands slipping under plaid pajamas and then she reminded me that we needed to get over for Christmas breakfast.

Everyone was still wearing their pajamas, and the parents looked a lot more tired than the kids did. There were mountains of presents under each tree, all marked with nametags. I was pretty sure I saw mine on at least one when I walked by.

Laura stopped me from walking into the dining room and pointed upward.

Right. Mistletoe. I guess it was probably really bad luck not to kiss under it on Christmas.

"Oh, what the hell." I grabbed her and she dipped me before laying a good one on me. Everyone in the dining room cheered and I forgot my own name as my head swam and Laura stuck her tongue in my mouth.

At last she let me up and I said in her ear, "I don't think tongue is part of the tradition."

"I was improvising," she said back.

We tried to go to our table, but everything was pushed together, so we all had to eat together.

"You two seem pretty cozy," Lillian said, giving me a look.

"We are," Laura said. "Cozy."

Lillian winked at both of us and put her finger to her lips as if she was keeping a secret.

Laura hadn't been exaggerating about the intensity of the Christmas breakfast. There was bread and eggs and potatoes and pancakes shaped like snowmen, fruit, croissants, Danishes, bacon, ham, and three kinds of quiche.

"I won't need to eat for a week after this," I said, loading up my plate.

I sat next to Laura as the dining room filled up with even more Sterlings who weren't staying at the inn, but had come for breakfast and presents. There were so many people that it was hard to have a conversation over all the noise of other people having conversations.

I stuffed my face and laughed with Laura and realized that I didn't want to leave. What harm was staying a few extra days? I didn't have to be back until the next Monday, so that was three extra days I could spend with the Sterlings. And with Laura.

I made the decision while I was eating and told Laura about it while everyone got together to open presents. The kids had a free-for-all and tore into their toys and the adults waited

Christmas Inn Maine

for the carnage to be over to pass out their presents. Someone also started the game of "looking for the Christmas pickle" ornament in the tree, which they were all having a great time looking for.

Lillian handed me a card and gave me a kiss on the cheek.

"Merry Christmas, Colden." I hugged her back and patted Minnie on the head.

The card was cute and inside was a printed page from my favorite online book retailer.

"Oh my god, thank you!" I hugged her again.

"I love the internet. You can buy anything on there. I don't even have to leave my house."

Lillian and I talked about the wonders of the internet and she told me about her Twitter account (which I immediately followed) and then Laina gave me another card and a present.

"Wow, thank you. You didn't have to do this on top of everything else."

I opened the present first. It was a Sterling Inn robe and slippers.

"Thank you so much. I love these robes." I immediately put it on and then opened the card.

"Now, that is a gift card to stay at The Sterling Inn for as long as you want, whenever you want, for the rest of your life." I turned the gift card over and it said "FREE STAYS FOREVER" and had Laina's signature.

I wanted to protest, yet again, that this was too much, but Laura pressed on my toes with her foot and gave me a look.

"Thank you. This means more than you can know." I hugged her and Antonio and probably every single other person in the Sterling family.

Laura ended up getting books and skincare products and concert tickets from her parents.

"There's two," she said, holding them up. They were for a band that I loved.

"Are you sure? Don't you have a friend you'd want to take?"

"The only person I want to take is you."

I accepted the ticket and a kiss.

"So much for discretion," I said.

"They already knew. All of them. They knew before we did. Or at least before you did."

I gave her a look.

"Did you know this was going to happen when I got here?"

"I mean, no, but I hoped. I really hoped. This has been the best Christmas ever."

It really had. I'd set out to have it alone, and here I was, part of a whole family.

Someone put on music and an epic cleanup started until a dance party broke out. Laura grabbed Lillian's hands and twirled her around the room. As I watched her, something happened to me.

Something big and scary and strange an unexpected.

I loved her. I did. There was no other word for this all-consuming feeling in my head and my heart and in every cell of my body.

I loved Laura Sterling. I loved her hard and I loved her deep and it had come upon me without a warning or indication.

I could try to deny it, but that would be foolish. She was going to read it all over my face. As if she'd heard me thinking about her, she danced over and grabbed my hand to swing me around. We laughed and danced and she swayed me back and forth.

I did a little shimmy move and she giggled.

"I love you," she said, and then realized what words had come out of her mouth. "Shit, I didn't mean to say that. I'm sorry. I didn't mean—"

"No, it's okay." I put my hand on her mouth and prepared

to make the best or worst mistake of my life. "I love you, Laura. I just realized it about five minutes ago, but I think it's been happening over this entire year. I fought it so hard, and I couldn't deny it anymore. Blame your freaking family for weakening my normally strong barriers against you. I guess it took seeing you here with them that just . . . I don't know. I love you."

She squealed and hugged me, spinning both of us around and around.

"I love you, Colden. I've loved you so long and you're so stubborn and I was convinced I was going to love your from afar for the rest of my life. But now I don't have to!" She swung me around and I screamed until she put me down.

"Merry Fucking Christmas, Colden," she said.

"Be careful. We probably shouldn't curse in front of the children." I glanced over at them, but they were all too engrossed in their toys to see what Laura and I were doing. "Never mind, they're not listening. Merry Fucking Christmas, Laura."

She kissed me without any mistletoe in front of her whole family and it was perfect. I'd gotten exactly what I'd wanted, if I'd known what to ask for.

Epilogue

"How are we going to do this?" I asked, as Laura and I stood outside the entrance to our office building holding hands. I'd stayed over at her place the night before and this was our first day back at work. I was already missing The Sterling Inn and everyone in it. Lillian had texted me twice already.

"We're going to be professional. We looked up the policy and since we're on the same level, there's no issue, but we should report it to HR. So that's what we'll do. And then . . . I'm not sure. The one thing I do know is that I love you." She gave me a quick kiss.

Laura and I had spent the entire drive back to Maine on the phone with each other, talking about how to make this thing work. I was fine with her calling me her girlfriend. I actually felt a little thrill of the idea of her claiming me that way, and me claiming her in return. I didn't know if I would always been okay with that term, but I'd cross that bridge when I got there.

"Oh, but I'm still going to throw you under the bus for a promotion. My career comes first," she said, and I pretended to shove her.

"You wouldn't dare."

"That's what you think." She pushed through the glass doors and I followed her to the elevator.

~

OUR MEETING with HR was quick and then we headed to our office. We'd agreed ahead of time that we should reserve any sort of couple things like kissing or cutesy nicknames for times outside of a professional environment. Plus, we didn't need to make our coworkers uncomfortable. I couldn't be that office asshole.

The rest of it, we'd have to figure out as we went along. It wasn't going to be easy, but we were doing it. The lease was up on my apartment in a few months, and I was already flirting with the idea of moving in with her. She definitely had the room and it was way too soon, but it was a possibility. I hadn't said anything to Laura yet, so I didn't scare her.

I was completely and utterly in love with her. More so than I ever knew was possible. Every day it grew and grew and I found new things about her that I adored. I also found new things about her that annoyed me, but that was all part of the package of being in love.

In love. I never thought it would happen to me, but here she was. I hadn't expected her, hadn't asked for her, but she was in my life and I wouldn't have it any other way. Our journey to get to each other was unconventional and not everyone understood it, but that didn't matter. As long as she loved me, and I loved her, I didn't care about what someone else thought.

"You're staring at me," she said, as I pretended to work on emails.

"I can't help it. You look really pretty today."

She tossed her hair over her shoulder.

"I look really pretty every day," she said.

I threw a paperclip at her.

"Hey, hostile work environment!"

We both smiled at each other and then I shook myself.

"Okay, back to work. Work. Working. Working now."

"Work now, fun later."

That caught my attention.

"What kind of fun?"

She wrote something on a sticky note and then held it up.

"Ohhhhhhh, *that* kind of fun."

She wiggled her eyebrows before tossing the sticky note in the trash.

"Just you wait, Colden. I've got plans."

"You always have plans." I tried to focus on the text on my screen, but it blurred and danced around. This was hopeless.

"Mmm, you love my plans," she said.

"A little bit, yeah."

I heard her fingers on the keys of her keyboard and I looked up to find her focused on her screen.

"What?" she said.

"Nothing."

"You're being really distracting, Colden. Remember? Work."

Right. Work. Being professional. Money. Career. I couldn't blow up my work life because of my love life.

She sighed heavily and I looked over at her.

"Sorry."

"No, it's okay."

Then she did it again.

"What?" I said.

"It's so long until we get to leave and normally I love being at work. This is a strange feeling. You're so close to me, but so far away. I'm not a fan." I wasn't either, but we were going to have to learn how to deal with it.

"How about I make out with you at lunch, will that help?"

She smiled brightly.

"Yup, that will *totally* work."

I didn't know how the next few days were going to go, or the next year, but all I knew was if she was at my side, we could do anything together. As long as she didn't try and steal my promotion. Then things were going to be a little awkward at home.

Somehow we made it through the day, and as soon as we left the building, our hands linked together as if they'd been pulled there by magnets.

"One day down, an eternity to go," she said as we swung our hands together.

"Eternity?" I asked. "Isn't it a little soon for that?"

"Some people take a lifetime to fall in love with someone else. We're just efficient in our time management. It didn't take us that long."

"Fair enough."

She stopped me on the sidewalk and kissed me.

"What was that for?" I asked when I caught my breath. Her kisses still made me weak in the knees.

"Couldn't help myself. Plus, it's a preview of what's happening later."

I looked around and very discreetly squeezed one of her boobs.

"What was that for?" she asked.

"Preview of what's happening later."

She burst out laughing and we kept walking toward her apartment.

READ JUST ONE NIGHT, **the first book in the Castleton Hearts series, available now!**

Afterword

Like this book? Reviews are SO appreciated! They can be long or short, or even just a star rating. Thank you so much!

Want another romance set in a small town Maine? Try The Girl Next Door!

Sign up for my newsletter for access to free books, sales, and up-to-date news on new releases!

Acknowledgments

Writing this book has been a roller coaster. I've had to squeeze it in moments between work, in between other projects, and in between yoga teacher training. It hasn't been easy, BUT, writing this book was pure joy. All I wanted was to write a book the way certain movies like *The Holiday* and *Last Holiday* made me feel. I wanted to see how many clichés I could fit in one book. Spot them all!

This is my first book with a nonbinary character. Colden is a demigirl, like me. If you've never heard of a demigirl, you're not alone! I hadn't heard of it a few years ago and now it's the word that best describes my gender. If you have any questions or are interested in learning more about being nonbinary, there are great resources online, and lots of people on twitter especially who share their experiences.

To be completely honest, I have been scared of writing this book all year, but in the end, it was much easier than I thought it would be. Colden's experience with her gender is not EXACTLY like mine because two people can never have the exact same experiences. Hers are drawn heavily from my own, though.

Thanks to everyone who told me how much they wanted this book, or were excited to read about a nonbinary character. I would not have had the courage to write this without you.

As always, thanks to my INCREDIBLE editor, Laura, who kills it every time and keeps me from making too big of an ass of myself.

Lastly, to all my nonbinary babes out there: I see you. I love you. I support you.

About the Author

Chelsea M. Cameron is a New York Times/USA Today Best Selling author from Maine who now lives and works in Boston. She's a red velvet cake enthusiast, obsessive tea drinker, vegetarian, former cheerleader and world's worst video gamer. When not writing, she enjoys watching infomercials, singing in the car, tweeting (this one time, she was tweeted by Neil Gaiman) and playing fetch with her cat, Sassenach. She has a degree in journalism from the University of Maine, Orono that she promptly abandoned to write about the people in her own head. More often than not, these people turn out to be just as

weird as she is. Connect with her on Twitter, Facebook, Instagram, Bookbub, Goodreads, and her Website.
If you liked this book, please take a few moments to **leave a review**. Authors really appreciate this and it helps new readers find books they might enjoy. Thank you!

Other books by Chelsea M. Cameron:

The Noctalis Chronicles
Fall and Rise Series
My Favorite Mistake Series
The Surrender Saga
Rules of Love Series
UnWritten
Behind Your Back Series
OTP Series
Brooks (The Benson Brothers)
The Violet Hill Series
Unveiled Attraction
Anyone but You
Didn't Stay in Vegas
Wicked Sweet
Christmas Inn Maine
Bring Her On
The Girl Next Door
Who We Could Be
Castleton Hearts Series

Christmas Inn Maine is a work of fiction. Names, characters, places and incidents are either the product of the author's imagination or are use fictiously. Any resemblance to actual persons, living or dead, events, business establishments or locales is entirely coincidental.

No part of this book may be reproduced, scanned or distributed in any printed or electronic form without permission. All rights reserved.

Copyright © 2019 Chelsea M. Cameron

Editing by Laura Helseth

Cover by Chelsea M. Cameron

Printed in Great Britain
by Amazon